"You're a real gr_____

"Sorry." Caroline turned her back. *Well, what a great start to senior year,* she thought. *If the rest of the year is going to be as bad as today, then I can't wait for graduation!*

"Are we still going to the park?" Tracy asked.

"There isn't time now. I'm going to the lunchroom."

Caroline led the way while Tracy followed in silence. Finally, Tracy spoke. "Cara, what's wrong? Tell me."

"Well," Caroline hesitated. "Okay. I guess it's better than brooding about it. I just can't believe you did that to me."

"Did what?"

"Gave Chrissy my job."

Tracy looked surprised. She took a seat next to Cara at a lunch table in the corner. "Look, I didn't mean to do that—I just thought having the job would help Chrissy get her mind off things."

"But you knew I was counting on it."

"But you said yourself you're not comfortable being a leader. I figured you and Chrissy would work together."

"I didn't want to work with Chrissy. I wanted to do it on my own."

Other books in the **SUGAR & SPICE** series:

\# 1 Two Girls, One Boy
\# 2 Trading Places
\# 3 The Last Dance
\# 4 Dear Cousin
\# 5 Nothing in Common
\# 6 Flip Side
\# 7 Tug of War
\# 8 Surf's Up!

COMING SOON

\#10 Make Me a Star
\#11 Big Sister

Janet Quin-Harkin's Sugar & Spice

Double Take

IVY BOOKS • NEW YORK

Ivy Books
Published by Ballantine Books
Copyright © 1987 by Butterfield Press, Inc. & Janet Quin-Harkin

Produced by Butterfield Press, Inc.
133 Fifth Avenue
New York, New York 10003

Library of Congress Catalog Card Number: 87-90997

ISBN 0-8041-0069-1

Manufactured in the United States of America

First Edition: January 1988

Double Take

Chapter 1

Caroline Kirby perched comfortably on the wide window seat in her room, and gazed down at the familiar scene before her. She really was lucky to live in San Francisco, she thought. No other place could possibly provide such a spectacular view.

Poor Chrissy, Caroline mused. *Soon she'll have to leave all this.* Behind her, Caroline could hear her cousin bustling about their bedroom, packing to go home to Iowa. *Was it only last summer that Chrissy had arrived here?* she wondered. After all they'd been through together this past year, Caroline felt as if she'd known Chrissy forever.

In fact, she hadn't even known of her cousin's existence until last summer when her mother had been reunited with Aunt Ingrid after many years apart. Aunt Ingrid had been worried that Chrissy was becoming too settled on the farm and would never have a chance to experience life anywhere else. *So good old Mom invited her to live with us for a year,* Caroline thought with a fond smile. *And to think I didn't want Chrissy to come! How different this year would have been!*

Sighing, Caroline peered at the distant waters of the San Francisco Bay, which sparkled in the afternoon sun. On the narrow streets below, cable cars chimed their warning bells, chugging up the steep hills of San Francisco. The jumble of colors and noises was never-ending—and never boring, as far as Caroline was concerned.

"Caroline, stop dreaming and help me do something with this mess!"

Chrissy stood in the middle of the room with her hands on her hips in helpless frustration, surrounded by heaps of clothing.

"*Mon Dieu,*" Caroline exclaimed as she surveyed the mess, "how did *that* happen?"

Across the room, Chrissy shoved damp bangs off her forehead. "Well for Pete's sake," Chrissy answered, dramatically throwing her hands in the air, "don't ask me. A minute ago this was *completely* organized."

"Why do I find that hard to believe?" There were about two dozen piles of things spilling over the bed and desk and nearly obliterating the floor. "Chrissy, all these piles just make things more confusing." Caroline leaped up. "Which stuff is which?"

Chrissy pointed. "Those piles are things to ship back home. These two piles are things to take on the plane, and . . ." She stopped in confusion. "And then I forget."

Caroline picked up a shoebox overflowing with trash. "First of all, throw your garbage out." She pulled out the wastebasket.

With a wild shriek, Chrissy sprang across the room, grabbing the box away. "Garbage?" she yelled. "These are souvenirs! Priceless memories!"

As Caroline stared in disbelief, Chrissy picked torn shreds of paper from the shoebox. "These are ticket stubs from all the movies I ever saw here. Remember how excited I was about the movies?"

"You couldn't believe there was more than one theater in town."

"Well, in Danbury we only have one theater and we're pretty lucky just to have that." Chrissy grinned. "I must have seen two hundred movies since I've been here."

Caroline stared in dismay. "And you saved every stub?"

Chrissy nodded. "It's a miracle I got any school work done at all."

"You almost didn't," Caroline reminded her. Carefully this time, Caroline plucked a plastic shopping bag from the floor. "And what precious memories are in here?"

"The most important ones," Chrissy swore. "That's my bag of letters from home."

Caroline hoisted the bag. "It's awfully heavy. Who wrote you so many letters besides your parents?"

"Well, you know Ben wrote me quite a few letters when I first got here," Chrissy began, "then he stopped writing after we broke up in April." She paused, her eyes taking on a sudden sparkle. "But since we saw each other in Hawaii a few weeks ago, I've been getting even more letters than ever!"

Caroline rolled her eyes. "Sounds like a soap opera."

"Well, I still haven't decided if I want to be more than just good friends," Chrissy remarked as she reached for the bag. Spilling crumpled envelopes onto the floor, she rummaged around, finally pulling out a rumpled, moldy-looking piece of gingham fabric. "Oh no!" she cried. "My costume from the school musical! I meant to wash it."

"Oh Chrissy!" Caroline collapsed on the window seat and hooted with laughter. "That was months ago!"

"Yuck." With the costume dangling from her fingers, Chrissy dashed down the hall to toss the outfit into the dirty clothes hamper. "Can you return it to school for me in September?" she asked Caroline a little sheepishly. "Tell Miss Barker I'm really sorry. I just forgot about it somehow."

"Never a dull moment." Caroline grinned and shook her head in exasperation. "Face it, Chrissy, you will never be an organized person."

"I guess not. If a year of living with you hasn't changed me," Chrissy admitted, "nothing could."

Fondly, Caroline looked at her cousin, then caught her own reflection in the bureau mirror behind Chrissy. With their long blond hair and blue eyes there was an unmistakable resemblance. "Chrissy, I'll never be the same without you. Think of everything we've been through together—the crazy adventures with boys, all the mix-ups and misunderstandings."

"Being camp counselors together," Chrissy added,

"our trip to Hawaii, the school musical, double-dating . . ."

"And liking each other's dates," Caroline reminded her.

Chrissy grinned. "Spending spring break in Danbury when you fell madly in love with Luke."

"It sure has been a wild year, hasn't it?" Caroline remarked. "I'm really going to miss you."

"I know." Chrissy sat on the window seat beside her cousin. "Me too." Suddenly she grinned. "But I have changed," she announced.

Caroline put an arm around her. "I hope not. You're great the way you are."

"For better or worse," Chrissy insisted, "I am no longer the country hick I was a year ago."

"You weren't such a hick," Caroline objected. "Even though I did expect you to be one. I thought you'd be some gawky farm girl with hay sticking out of her ears, terrified of the big city."

"I was pretty terrified," Chrissy said.

"You didn't act it."

"I was." Suddenly, Chrissy looked worried. "Caroline, I haven't been—I haven't been too hard to live with, have I? I mean . . ." she hesitated.

"I know exactly what you mean," Caroline said. She paused thoughtfully. Where she was neat, Chrissy was messy. Where she was quiet and reserved, Chrissy was all bouncy good spirits. Where she was cautious, Chrissy acted first and thought later—if at all. To be honest, there were times in the past year when Caroline thought she'd lose her mind. Sharing her room—and her life—with her unpredictable cousin was the hardest thing she'd ever done. Still . . . Suddenly Caroline grinned.

"I had more fun this year than I've had in my entire life!"

As the two cousins hugged, Caroline felt tears well up in her eyes. It was true—for all the trouble and misunderstandings, she had grown to love her cousin like a sister. She almost couldn't imagine living without her.

"Cara, don't cry," Chrissy said softly. "We'll write loads of letters—enough to fill ten bags. And we'll visit each other on vacations."

Caroline nodded and sniffled, but didn't say anything. Then she noticed a tear trickling down Chrissy's face too.

"Oh rats," Chrissy said, wiping the tear away. "Between the two of us we'll flood out all of San Francisco!"

Caroline gave a weak smile, then took a deep breath and pulled herself together. "Come on, let's get you packed," she told her cousin.

An hour later, Caroline had organized Chrissy's things into half a dozen neatly packed cartons labeled *For Storage*, *To Be Shipped Later*, and *Pack for Plane*.

Satisfied, she surveyed the restored order of the bedroom. Sad as she was about Chrissy's leaving, she couldn't suppress a wild spurt of elation. She was getting her room back again! After a year of living side-by-side, it was too good to be true—a whole room to herself! A whole closet, a whole bureau, all her bookshelves, and every shelf in the bathroom! Paradise!

The first things to go would be the extra bed and

dresser, Caroline thought. Her parents would probably squawk about losing the storage space, but
after all, this would be her senior year, probably
her last year living at home. She deserved to have
her room exactly how she wanted it. She'd sacri-
ficed a lot to share with Chrissy—and now she
could make up for lost time.

She felt Chrissy looking at her strangely. "Penny
for your thoughts," Chrissy said.

Caroline flushed. *Chrissy's still here and I'm already planning the great things I'll do without her!*

"I, uh, was thinking how different things will be,
from now on," she replied, avoiding her cousin's
gaze.

Chrissy nodded thoughtfully. "I have to admit I
was thinking how great it will be to get home and
have my own room again!"

Caroline stared. It always amazed her that
Chrissy could say exactly what was on her mind!

"Well, actually," she confessed, "I was sort of
thinking the same thing."

Chrissy laughed out loud. "We're cousins, all
right. We even think alike!"

Caroline smiled back. "Listen, Chrissy—what do
you think of my decorating scheme?" Excitedly,
Caroline described her plans for her made-over
bedroom. No more little girl look. She'd pack away
her stuffed animals—well, most of them—and leave
only a few choice objects on the shelves. Instead of
a bulletin board crowded with pictures, she would
have well-designed posters from art museums and
galleries.

"It'll be very sleek and modern," Caroline enthused. "Ultra-sophisticated—what a high school senior should have."

"Not me," Chrissy promptly declared. "I'm gonna plaster my room with all my mementos. You know the first thing I'm gonna do when I get home?" She answered her own question without giving Caroline a chance to respond. "Hang up every souvenir from San Francisco I got this year, and then throw a huge bash—the biggest party Danbury ever saw. Invite everyone I know! I don't want to be forgotten my senior year."

Caroline laughed. Who could forget Chrissy!

"Don't worry," she assured her cousin, "you'll be as popular as ever. Knowing you, you'll probably get yourself into another ridiculous mess the instant you get off the plane. If you can wait that long!"

There was a soft knock on the door. "Can I come in?"

"Sure, Mom." Caroline opened the door for her mother. "We've finally got Chrissy's things organized."

Her mother entered the room, looking distracted and grim. Caroline and Chrissy exchanged a puzzled look.

"Don't worry, Aunt Edith," Chrissy reassured her, "there's less than it looks. We can ship it home easily. We worked awfully hard sorting it out."

Wearily, Caroline's mother sat on the edge of the bed. "I'm afraid, girls, your hard work was for nothing."

"What do you mean?" Chrissy asked.

Caroline sat down next to her mother. "Mom, is something wrong?"

"I'm afraid so." Sadly, Edith Kirby shook her head. "Chrissy, I just spoke with your mother on the phone, and it's pretty bad news. Your family . . ."

"Oh no," Chrissy shrieked, flinging her hands over her ears. "Don't tell me! Something horrible has happened. I knew it. I just knew everything was going too good to be true!" She threw herself across the bed.

"Chrissy!" Alarmed, Caroline tugged at her cousin's arms. "Chrissy, you don't even know what it is!"

Caroline turned to her mother. "Mom, it's not Aunt Ingrid, is it? Or the boys or Uncle . . ."

Her mother took Caroline's hands. "They're all okay," she assured her.

"Then . . . what?"

Gently, Mrs. Kirby released Caroline and laid a hand on Chrissy's head. Chrissy sat up, but her eyes were screwed tightly closed and she refused to take her fingers out of her ears.

"A tornado," Caroline's mother said simply. "Chrissy's family's house—it's gone. There's nothing left. Nothing at all."

Caroline let out a loud gasp. A tornado!

Chrissy's eyes grew wide and she opened her mouth as if to speak, but no words came out. Then she buried her face in the pillow and began punching it with both hands. "No, not a twister!" she cried, over and over. "It can't be. It just can't be!"

Too stunned to react, Caroline stared at her mother. *It's a terrible joke—some cruel, terrible joke! It isn't true. It just can't be true!*

"I'm sorry, Chrissy," Edith Kirby said softly. "The tornado just struck your house the hardest."

"Mom," Caroline said, "the rest of the town . . ."

"Hit, but not as badly," her mother assured her. "There were no fatalities—thank goodness for that—but there was a lot of damage."

Chrissy snapped to attention. "Omigosh—Ben! Is he—his family . . . and Grandma Madden, she's okay, isn't she?"

"And Luke," Caroline added in a tight voice. Her whole body felt suddenly cold with fear.

"They're okay," Mrs. Kirby said. "Your mother said not to worry about anyone."

"But the house," Chrissy said slowly, "it's . . . all gone?"

"I'm afraid so."

Chrissy stared blindly ahead of her, while Caroline tried to imagine what her cousin must be feeling. She knew that Chrissy had lived in that house since the day she was born, and everything in it was special to her—from the large dining room table where the Maddens ate all their meals, to the old-fashioned quilts Grandma Hansen had made years ago. Some things could be replaced, but for other things there were no substitutes.

Just imagine—no more family snapshots, no special birthday cards or Valentines, Caroline thought, *no records or books or . . . anything. It was all blown away!*

Chrissy must have been thinking the same thing, for Caroline had never seen her look so mournful.

She moaned softly. "Everything's gone. I can't believe it! But how did it happen, Aunt Edith? Where was everyone when it hit? Golly, it must have been awful."

Her aunt put an arm around her shoulders.

"Luckily, the whole family was away. Your father needed some new parts for the tractor and at the last minute they all decided to go and make a day of it."

"How lucky," Caroline exclaimed.

Chrissy seemed to be in a state of shock. "Then it was just fate that they weren't . . ."

Mrs. Kirby nodded. "It was fate, all right. As a special treat, Ingrid and Richard took the boys to a movie that night. They were just about to head home when they heard the tornado warning. Lots of people were in the same position, so the Red Cross opened an emergency shelter in a local school overnight. Your dad wanted to head back to the farm, to do what he could, but the other people there talked him out of it."

"Thank goodness!" Caroline felt a shiver of fear.

"In the morning," her mother continued, "they went home. The area was a mess and the farm was demolished."

Chrissy merely shook her head, looking stunned. Caroline didn't blame her—it was hard to comprehend such a loss, and to realize how close the Maddens had come to grave danger.

Chrissy sprang off the bed. "I've got to call them. See if they're all right. I'll have to go home right away."

"Wait, Chrissy." Mrs. Kirby held her back. "They're not at home, remember?" She spoke extra gently, as if to a frightened child.

Chrissy looked puzzled, but then sank back down on the bed. "Oh. I forgot. There isn't any home." She dropped her head into her hands.

Caroline felt a sharp pang of horror. "Oh,

Chrissy!" She went to her cousin and enfolded her in a giant hug. If it had been her home, Caroline thought, she would be collapsed in tears. But as she hugged her cousin, she felt Chrissy's inner strength returning.

Chrissy shook herself and straightened her shoulders. "My poor mom," she murmured, "and the kids . . . what they must be . . . Where are they, Aunt Edith? How can I . . . ?"

"They're at your Uncle Ned's."

"Uncle Ned! But he lives in another county. That's so far away. Why aren't they staying with someone in town?"

"Chrissy, I wrote your uncle's number on the pad by the phone in my room," her aunt said. "Why don't you call your parents there? You'll feel better."

Chrissy nodded. "I guess I will."

"Good luck, honey." With a worried expression, Caroline's mother gave Chrissy's arm a little squeeze.

"I hope she's all right," Caroline said.

Her mother sighed. "She didn't give me a chance to tell her—oh well, maybe it's best coming from her own mother, anyway."

"Tell her what? Mom, what is it," Caroline asked in alarm. "You're not hiding something, are you? Not more bad news?"

Her mother gave her a sharp look. "Don't you go falling to pieces. We have to be strong for Chrissy. No, Caroline, it's not more bad news. One disaster is enough for this family!"

"Then what is it?"

"It's just that . . ." Her mother hesitated. Caroline

felt a wild urge to shake her. She was desperate to hear the news.

"Chrissy doesn't know it, but she won't be going home."

Caroline stared. "What do you mean?"

"Don't look so alarmed. But her family is staying at Uncle Ned's permanently. Or at least until they figure out a better alternative. No one in town could help them—they've all got damage of their own to content with."

"Even so, I can't believe no one would help," she said quietly. "Why can't Chrissy stay with a family in town? She has friends."

"Frankly, honey, no one made such an offer. People there have enough on their hands, even without a tornado hitting. None of them are particularly well-off."

"I guess, but still . . . Not even Ben's family?"

"They may have offered. But I don't think Chrissy's parents would like that idea anyway. They wouldn't want to put anyone out at a time like this, and with Chrissy and Ben at a crossroads in their relationship, it might be uncomfortable."

"I guess," Caroline said doubtfully. "But it doesn't seem fair. Poor Chrissy! Shipped off to her Uncle Ned's. Now she'll have to spend senior year in another new school. What a lousy break."

Caroline's mother gave her a puzzled look. "Cara—I'm surprised at you. You're missing the point. Chrissy isn't going to her uncle's. I wouldn't hear of it."

"She's not?" Caroline asked. "But I thought you said that Aunt Ingrid and everyone are staying at their Uncle Ned's."

"They are, but Chrissy's Uncle Ned already has a house full of kids, and since Chrissy is already used to living here . . ."

Now Caroline felt a new kind of shock. "Wait a minute!"

Here? she thought. *Chrissy's staying?* Caroline knew that was what her mother meant, but the idea just wasn't penetrating her brain. All the memories of the good times she'd had with her cousin this past year suddenly vanished. She knew it was selfish of her, but she didn't want Chrissy to stay.

"It's the most logical solution," her mother went on. "I've discussed it with Ingrid and she agrees. Chrissy isn't going anywhere because she's staying here. She'll finish high school at Maxwell with you, and all her new friends. I think it's the best way."

Caroline nodded, forcing a smile. "Of course. I'll . . . I'll go tell Chrissy how . . . glad I am."

I can't believe it! Here I was so excited about getting my room back to myself! Looking forward to senior year on my own. And now . . . now Chrissy isn't going home after all!

Chapter 2

Caroline hesitated and knocked softly on the door to the master bedroom. Inside, Chrissy was sprawled across the bed, dissolved in tears, holding the phone in one hand.

"Okay, Mom. I understand. I love you too, Mom, all of you. I will. I . . . goodbye."

For once, Chrissy seemed spiritless—absolutely, totally crushed—as she hung up the phone. Caroline had never seen her looking so devastated, and her heart went out to Chrissy. She had grown to love her cousin, and Chrissy had become a big part of her life. Sure she would have missed not having Chrissy around, yet she preferred that to putting up with her cousin for another year.

Still, she *did* love her cousin. *And now's a good*

time to tell her so—she needs to hear it more than ever, Caroline thought.

Sitting on the bed, Caroline gently stroked Chrissy's shaking shoulders. "Don't cry, Chrissy . . . I'll help, if I can."

"Oh, Caroline . . ." with a heartbreaking sob, Chrissy collapsed in her cousin's arms.

"Shh, everything will be all right Chrissy. You'll see," Caroline comforted. But tears welled in her own eyes as she smoothed Chrissy's blond hair back from her splotchy, tear-stained face.

Caroline was shaken. She had seen her cousin in every mood from carefree to angry to dejected, but never as helpless and devastated as this. But then, Chrissy had never experienced such a dreadful loss before.

"Oh, Chrissy, I feel so badly for you," Caroline said softly. "I wish I could do something to make you feel better."

Chrissy wiped her eyes, but fresh tears spilled down her cheeks. "I—I'll be all right," she gulped. "It's the shock . . ."

"I know, I know," Caroline soothed. "Don't worry, everything will be all right."

Chrissy shook herself loose from Caroline's grip. "I know that. I also know that I'm not the one suffering most. My poor Mom—it nearly broke my heart to hear her cry. Our beautiful house—and the animals, most of them are still missing." Her eyes misted over. "At least my dog is okay. I don't know what I would have done if anything had happened to Bonnie."

Bravely, Chrissy forced a laugh. "Look at me—I won't do anybody any good this way." Plucking some tissues from the bedside table, she dried her eyes and blew her nose.

"Did your mom tell you," Caroline began, and then hesitated. She wasn't exactly sure how to break the news, if Chrissy didn't already know. "About your . . . not going home . . ."

"Yes," Chrissy said simply. "And it really hurts. That's the worst part of all—not being able to rush right home. Caroline, I know it's dumb—even morbid—but I wish I could see it! I know the house isn't really there anymore, but . . ."

"I think I understand," Caroline said slowly. "I guess unless you see for yourself, you can't really believe that something so awful could have happened."

Chrissy nodded. "And maybe I could find something . . . just one of the knick-knacks from my room, a scrap of wallpaper maybe . . . anything from the house that I could save."

"I'm sure your mom will do that for you."

"How? How can she when she's miles and miles away? My Uncle Ned doesn't live anywhere near Danbury!"

Caroline was silent. She could only imagine how awful Chrissy must feel, how alone. "If it helps," she offered, "I'm sure Mom would let you call Ben if you wanted, or some of your other friends back home. You might feel better, talking it over with a friend."

"Oh, I'll call Ben today, that's for sure," Chrissy agreed, "and maybe some others. It seems everyone else got away lucky. The tornado blew off some roofs, but at least their houses are still standing."

"Chrissy—I know how I would feel if this had

happened to me and my family—well, I just think it's okay for you to feel angry. I mean, you must be wondering, why your house and not someone else's—it's only human."

"I do feel that way, a little," Chrissy admitted. "Though I'm really glad my friends' houses are okay, and Ben's, of course— but I just can't believe this has happened to me."

"I think you're taking it awfully well," Caroline said sincerely. "I'd be a basket case."

"And I'm not?" Chrissy asked. She got up from the bed and crossed the room to look at herself in the mirror. Her eyes were rimmed with red and her T-shirt was smudged with tears. To top it off, a thatch of straw-colored hair stood straight up on top of her head. "If I'm not a basket case, I don't know what is," she said with a shake of her head.

"You're right. I take it back," Caroline agreed with a grin. "Well, come on and I'll help you put your things away. After you make your phone calls, that is."

"Yeah—I guess I'd better unpack. After all, I'll be here another week or two."

"Another week or two!" Caroline stared at her. "Chrissy, I thought you knew. Didn't your mother tell you the arrangements?"

"Of course." Chrissy started to dial the phone. "Ben first, then my grandmother. You're sure it's okay to run up your phone bill?"

"Chrissy—I don't think you understand."

Chrissy gave her an almost normal smile. "Sure I do, Caroline. I can't say I'm happy about it. Imagine, asking me to stay away for a while. That's like asking a—a bear to stay away from honey. Or a hog from mud, or a . . ."

Caroline took the phone from Chrissy's hand and hung it up.

"Now what'd you do that for?" Chrissy asked, obviously annoyed.

"You don't understand. Your mom didn't mean for you to stay here a week or two." Chrissy's eyes were so trusting that Caroline almost didn't have the heart to explain. She took a deep breath. "Chrissy, you're not going home *at all.*"

Chrissy laughed—a weak, half-hearted laugh. "You're just kidding, right?"

Quickly, Caroline explained that Chrissy's folks felt it was better for Chrissy to stay in San Francisco and finish her senior year at Maxwell High.

"I don't believe you," Chrissy cried when she had finished. "They'd never say that! They want me home as much as I . . ." Shocked, she stared at Caroline for a full minute. Caroline had absolutely no idea what to say.

"I'm sorry, Chrissy," she finally murmured. "I know you were really looking forward to being home again . . ."

"Looking forward," Chrissy shrieked. "I couldn't wait, that's all! Senior year back in my own house, with my own family and friends—I can't stay! I won't! I just can't stay here another whole year!"

"Chrissy, you don't have a choice," Caroline said. "Besides, it's not that bad here, is it?" she added in a joking voice.

"Oh, I didn't mean it that way. Gosh, you know what I mean. As nice as you all are—as much as I love San Francisco—this isn't home, Caroline. I thought . . ." With a moan, Chrissy threw herself back across the bed.

"Well, I really am sorry, Chrissy," Caroline said. "I guess . . . I guess I'll leave you alone for a while."

Shutting the door behind her, Caroline went back to her room to think. Her mind was in a whirl.

Admit it, Caroline Kirby, you're angry.

It was true. It sounded terrible, but Chrissy had some nerve complaining about staying in Caroline's house! She should be grateful she had a place to stay!

Caroline kicked a carton aside and plopped angrily on her bed. *Drat Chrissy's messes!* Suddenly the awful reality of it struck her: another whole year of sharing her room with Chrissy. With Chrissy's endless piles of junk. Another year of making compromises. Another twelve months of grin-and-bear it when things got tense.

It seemed cold-hearted and mean, but Caroline honestly didn't know if she could take it.

I don't think I want Chrissy to stay, she decided. *I've been looking forward to her going home. I don't think I can live this way another year.*

But Chrissy had nowhere else to go. *How can I even think these things?* Feeling angry and ashamed, Caroline bolted from her room, slamming the door behind her.

In the kitchen, she put a kettle of water on to boil. A nice cup of tea would help her think straight. She needed to calm down. Her mother entered as Caroline was pouring a splash of milk into her cup. "Want some, Mom?"

"That would be nice." Her mother sat near her. "Honey, I know it's not the most appropriate time to discuss this, but I saw some wonderful wall units on sale yesterday. We could get them for your room, to give the two of you a bit more space for your things. That should ease the clutter."

"It's Chrissy's clutter, not mine," Caroline grumbled.

"Caroline!"

"Well, I'm sorry, but no one's said a word about how I might feel having Chrissy here for another year. I get most of the responsibility, but nobody even *asked* me."

Her mother looked at her sharply. "I'm disappointed in you, Cara. I didn't think you still resented having your cousin here. I thought you really liked Chrissy. I thought you two were like sisters now."

"I do like her and I'm used to having her around. I would have missed her a lot—but Mom, it's my senior year! Maybe my last year at home. That means I'll never have my room to myself again before going away to college."

"It's just a room, Caroline. It shouldn't matter that much."

"But it does matter. I'm not trying to be selfish. I don't know, maybe if Chrissy had her own room or something . . ." Caroline suggested.

"That's not very generous. Or realistic."

"Mom, I know. I realize it's not the worst thing in the world. Some kids share all their lives. It's just that Chrissy and I are so different."

"Some of those differences are good," her mother said. "Even you admit you've loosened up with Chrissy around."

"That's true, but now I want to be on my own again. Without Chrissy," Caroline stressed. "Can't you see it my way? Oh, Mom . . ."

Chrissy appeared in the doorway, oblivious of the strained atmosphere in the room. Her eyes were extra bright and her color had returned.

"I just want to make an announcement. I know no one expected things to work out this way, but since they have . . ." She faltered for a moment, then her words picked up speed. "Since they have, and I'm going to be living here another year, then I am devoting this year to San Francisco and Maxwell High. It'll be the best year any Senior ever had!"

Before anyone could say a word, she bounced out of the room, leaving Caroline and her mother staring in surprise.

"Chrissy," Caroline's mother called, "where are you going?"

"To unpack for good," Chrissy said with determination.

Her mother poured hot water into her teacup. "Chrissy is a real trooper," she said. "I'd like to say the same about you, Cara. It would be nice if you helped her unpack."

"I just packed her," Caroline muttered.

"Well, I'm sure she could use some cheering up. Now wipe that frown off your face and stop feeling sorry for yourself."

Caroline glared at her mother, then grabbed her cup and spilled the rest of her tea into the sink. Some comfort!

Perfect. Even my own mother is against me, she thought moodily. *Thanks a lot, Chrissy!*

In the bedroom, Chrissy was a whirlwind of activity. Her face shone with feverish excitement as she tossed her belongings every which way.

"Isn't it great, Cara?" Smash! Her tennis racket landed against the wall. "Think of all the wonderful things we can do together now!" Crash! Her collection of cute stuffed animals went flying into the closet. "I'll organize it later," Chrissy murmured. "We never did take that tour of Alcatraz, and there's the ferry to Sausalito—we can go two or three more times! And I'm dying to hike the whole of Mount Tamalpais. There's no *end* to the things we can do together."

The more she raved, the more sullen Caroline felt. "Great," she drawled.

"Help me with these things, Cara."

For the next forty minutes, Chrissy handed things to Caroline and Caroline made a valiant effort to put them away neatly. It was a hopeless cause. By the time Chrissy had everything out of the cartons, the room was as cluttered and messy as ever.

As Chrissy handed her the last shopping bag, Caroline was nearly pouting. Suddenly Chrissy's eyes filled with tears again.

"What now," Caroline asked.

"These letters from home," Chrissy gulped. Caroline recognized the stack of letters they had discussed earlier. "They're all I have left. Everything else from home is gone."

"Oh Chrissy, I am sorry," Caroline said truthfully.

But suddenly Chrissy shifted into high gear again, bathing Caroline with a radiant smile. "Oh well. No use crying over spilt milk! Better push your books over, Cara—I'll need every inch of space on that shelf."

With a sigh, Caroline cleared off half of her bookshelf again. So much for her redecorating scheme. *Goodbye, sophisticated new look. Hello, Chrissy's mess. Welcome home!*

Chapter 3

Caroline leaned against a bulletin board out of the way of the crowd in the corridor. After the months of summer vacation, the halls at Maxwell High seemed more busy and bustling than ever. There was the usual scramble to find classrooms and the usual confusion over new schedules. But for once, Caroline wasn't paralyzed with first-day-of-school anxiety. In between her morning classes she had laughed and chatted and exchanged stories with friends she hadn't seen since June. All in all, she was feeling pretty proud of herself.

I really have changed, Caroline realized. *Last year, I was all nervous and uptight on the first day. It's still a bit confusing, but I know I can handle it now. If I could handle a bunkful of crazy kids at camp this summer, I can handle anything.*

Just then someone called her name. Caroline

looked up to see Tracy Wong hurrying toward her. As always, her friend's glossy dark hair swung at her shoulders and her clothes looked fresh and neat, but her usually merry, almond eyes looked worried.

"Cara! Where've you been?"

Breathlessly, Tracy piled into Caroline, nearly knocking her over. "I thought you were coming to the park for lunch!"

"I'm on my way now," Caroline said, amused at Tracy's distress. "My English class ran late—first day enthusiasm. Look at this homework assignment!" She held up a notebook.

"That's tough," Tracy groaned in commiseration. "Poor Cara. Sorry I panicked, but the thought of eating alone, especially first day . . . You know how it is."

"Sure I do." Caroline began walking down the hall toward the door. "Let's go together."

"Oh wait, look at that." Tracy pointed to the bulletin board above Caroline's head where someone had hung a brightly painted poster.

"Sign up for Senior Activity Committee," Caroline read out loud. "Great! I can't believe I almost missed this poster. I'm so glad you saw it! Look, Tracy." She flipped through her notebook and showed Tracy a neatly-lettered list.

"Senior Game Show. Senior Beach Blanket Bingo Party. Senior Barbecue. Silly Pet Show. Mount Tamalpais Challenge Climb," Tracy recited. She wrinkled her nose. "More homework? I don't get it."

"Those are my suggestions for senior activities."

"Great, but what are you going to do with them?

No one even knows who the chairman is yet," Tracy pointed out.

"Chairperson," Caroline corrected. "Anyway, I'm not giving them to anyone. Actually, I thought I might be head of the committee."

"You?" Tracy looked mildly shocked. "Well, that's a good idea, Cara, but I didn't think you'd want to be *in charge* of the committee."

"Don't forget the organizing I did last year to save our park from being destroyed," Caroline reminded her friend.

"And a good thing too," Tracy remarked. "I'd hate to eat lunch in a parking garage."

Caroline grinned. "Well, I thought about it a lot this summer, and I decided. I really *can* do things like that when I put my mind to it. Mom's right—it's good for me to get involved in school activities."

"And it only took you 'til senior year to find that out," Tracy teased.

Caroline nodded seriously. "I know. And I'm not saying it will be easy, especially as I'm not usually very comfortable being the leader of a group. But this is for the good of the class. And you know, Tracy," she said excitedly, "I think I have some pretty good ideas."

As she and Tracy re-read the list, two more friends joined them.

"Look who made it through the summer in one piece," Justine remarked, running a slender hand through her long, blond hair.

"Hi, Justine," Caroline greeted her, as she secretly admired the other girl's stylish outfit. "How was your summer?"

"On a scale of one to ten, I'd give it an eleven," Justine said.

"She met a college boy, can you believe it?" Maria piped up, her brown eyes sparkling. "They spent every minute together."

"And how was *your* summer, Maria?" Caroline turned her attention to the dark-haired girl, giving her a warm smile.

"Not as hot as Justine's, but I managed." Grinning, she gave Caroline's arm a friendly squeeze. "Let's eat lunch together, and I'll fill you in."

"Great! I just want to put my name down on this sign-up sheet." Caroline dug in her purse for a pen.

"Senior Activity Committee?" Maria gazed at the poster thoughtfully. "Sounds like a lot of work. That stuff's not for me. I'll sign up for the Having Fun Committee."

Caroline smiled. "If they name me chairperson, I'll put that on the agenda."

Even Justine laughed at Caroline's joke. "Good luck," she said. "But I wonder who else wants the job? I agree with Maria—too much work."

Tracy grabbed Caroline's arm. "Look, everybody," she said in a lowered voice. "Here comes Chrissy! I've hardly seen her since . . . you know, the bad news. I feel so sorry for the poor kid—it's awful, what happened to her family."

"But she's taking it well," Maria said. "Isn't she, Cara?"

"I guess so," Caroline said.

Chrissy approached the group with a big smile. "Hi, everyone," she greeted them brightly. "Where've you all been? There's no one but strangers in my classes this year."

"Don't worry," Maria assured her. "Didn't we both sign up for 20th Century Lit. with Ms. Kranepool? That's the last class of the day."

"Great!" Chrissy smiled even wider. She nodded at the poster on the bulletin board. "Is this what you're all looking at? What's it about?"

"Senior Activities Committee," Tracy explained. "Show her your list, Cara."

Reluctantly, Caroline handed the piece of paper to Chrissy. For some reason she couldn't explain, she felt a sense of dread sharing her ideas with her cousin.

Chrissy looked at the list thoughtfully. "You thought of these things?"

"They're just rough ideas," Caroline told her quickly. "Some major activities and some smaller ones, just to get the ball rolling. I think class spirit is especially important for Seniors and I . . ."

"You're right there," Chrissy agreed, "but all of these take lots of time to plan. Why don't we have some activities that we can plan for the next few weeks to drum up senior spirit?"

"Like what?" Tracy asked.

"I don't know. A picnic at school? Or a coffee hour, or something like that. Or," Chrissy's eyes lit up and Caroline could imagine her mind racing, "what about a weekly coffee hour? You could make it a working meeting for your committee—a brainstorming session. That way you'd get kids to contribute ideas and have fun at the same time."

"What a good idea," Justine said, giving Chrissy a look of admiration.

"Well, I thought . . ." Caroline put in.

Tracy patted Chrissy's back. "Chrissy, you'd make a great committee chairman!"

Caroline felt stunned. A minute ago, Tracy thought that she should have the job!

"Chairperson," Chrissy corrected, glancing at Caroline for approval.

"I mean it," Tracy said. "No one has more energy than you."

Chrissy shrugged. "I don't know. Me, running such an important committee?"

"This class could use some fresh energy," Justine said.

Chrissy nodded thoughtfully. "I've got plenty of that. And I do believe in class spirit."

"You'd be great," Maria said.

"You know, back home I could have been head cheerleader. But that's not going to happen now . . ." Briefly, Chrissy looked despondent.

"Exactly why you should do this," Tracy encouraged her. "You like being involved."

"Maybe you're right. I should be part of this." Reaching up, Chrissy signed her name.

"Don't sign at the bottom," Justine told her, "sign at the top. You should be chairperson."

"Justine's right," Maria said.

"Oh, I don't know, Maria. People might not want a . . . a newcomer."

The whole crowd hooted except for Caroline. "You're no newcomer," Maria exclaimed. "You're one of us! Isn't she, Cara?"

"Absolutely." Caroline smiled stiffly.

"Do you really think so, Cara?" Chrissy waited for an answer, but Tracy interrupted.

"We *all* think you'd be great. Besides," she hesitated, "well, it would be good for you. It would take your mind off things. Right, Cara?"

Caroline shifted uneasily under Tracy's gaze. She had wanted so badly to run the committee herself. "Uh, it isn't really up to us, is it? I mean, you can't just appoint yourself chairperson."

"No, but Mr. Wells is the committee adviser," Justine told them all. "If we all went to him and said Chrissy's the best one for the job, I bet he'd consider it."

Chrissy's eyes began dancing. "You really want me to do it?"

"Are you kidding? You'd be great," Maria said.

"Do it, Chrissy," Tracy urged.

Chrissy turned to Caroline. Caroline felt a leap of hope—maybe Chrissy would suggest that they share the honors. That would be almost as good as running the committee herself.

"Cara, can I borrow your list? It could help give me ideas. I think I should have some definite plans before anybody talks to Mr. Wells."

"Oh, uh ... sure, fine," Caroline stammered. Cheeks flaming, she tore the paper from her notepad and handed it to Chrissy.

"Thanks a heap. Golly, I'm so thrilled you guys want me to do it!" Chrissy said, beaming.

Justine wrote out an informal petition endorsing Chrissy as Senior Activities Committee Chairman and had everyone in the group sign it, along with several passersby in the hallway.

"We've got plenty of names," she exclaimed. "Let's go see Mr. Wells now, before anyone else gets the idea of being chairperson."

"Great idea."

Chrissy, Justine, and Maria turned to go. "Oh, wait a minute," Chrissy said. "Caroline—are you still going to sign up? It would be fun to have you on my committee."

"Of course she is," Tracy said.

"Actually, Chrissy, you already have enough people," Justine pointed out.

"Well, the more the merrier," Maria said.

Caroline tried not to let them see how upset she was. Being part of Chrissy's committee was not exactly what she'd had in mind, but how could she say no without hurting Chrissy's feelings? She hesitated, then thought of a perfect excuse. "Oh, uh—I was also thinking of, uh, taking acting classes," she improvised. "Uh, after school, maybe. So I might not have time after all."

"Wow!" Maria looked impressed. "Are these acting classes going to take the place of your ballet lessons? Are you aiming to be a movie star now instead of a prima ballerina?"

"Well, I might." Caroline felt Tracy looking at her strangely.

"I didn't know that. Since when?" Tracy demanded.

"I've been considering it for a while," Caroline mumbled. "And now is the perfect time to start classes."

"It s a surprise to me," Tracy said.

It's a surprise to me, too. Caroline moved away from the group. "If I don't grab lunch now, I'll never eat," she told them.

"Sure, we understand," Justine told her. "Anyway, it's too bad you won't be on the committee with Chrissy. I think I may even sign up."

"Fabulous," Chrissy gushed.

"Bye, Cara," Maria said. "We'll have that lunch tomorrow, okay?"

"See you on the silver screen," Justine called.

"This is going to be a great committee," Caroline heard Maria saying as the three girls hurried down the hall.

"You should have gone with them," Tracy said.

"Committees aren't my thing," Caroline snapped.

"But you were so excited about it."

Caroline stared at Tracy in disbelief. "I don't get it! You were the one who said Chrissy would make a great chairperson!" she exclaimed.

"So, what's that got to do with you?"

"If you don't know, I'm not going to tell you," Caroline said moodily.

"You're a real grouch today."

"Sorry." Caroline turned her back. *Well, what a great start to senior year,* she thought. *If the rest of the year is going to be as bad as today, then I can't wait for graduation!*

"Are we still going to the park?" Tracy asked.

"There isn't time now. I'm going to the lunchroom."

Caroline led the way while Tracy followed in silence. Finally, Tracy spoke. "Cara, what's wrong? Tell me."

"Well," Caroline hesitated. "Okay. I guess it's better than brooding about it. I just can't believe you did that to me."

"Did what?"

"Gave Chrissy my job."

Tracy looked surprised. She took a seat next to Cara at a lunch table in the corner. "Look, I didn't mean to do that—I just thought having the job would help Chrissy get her mind off things."

"But you knew I was counting on it."

"But you said yourself you're not comfortable being a leader. I figured you and Chrissy would work together."

"I didn't want to work with Chrissy. I wanted to do it on my own."

"Oh. I guess I did get carried away," Tracy said apologetically. She suddenly smiled. "But it doesn't matter—not if you'd rather take acting classes."

"I don't even know where that came from," Caroline admitted. "I only said that so Chrissy wouldn't feel bad about squeezing me out."

"I feel terrible." Tracy said, looking down at the lunch in front of her. "I didn't mean to hurt you."

"That's okay." Caroline picked at her sandwich. She had no appetite at all.

"You could tell Chrissy how you feel."

"I'd look like a jerk. Everyone would think I was just jealous."

"This is a tough one."

"Forget it." Caroline tore a bite out of her apple. "It's too late now."

"You were really nice—not to tell Chrissy how you felt," Tracy said warmly.

"But I don't want to be nice," Caroline confessed. "I—I can't stand Chrissy for getting the job I wanted!" Tracy looked shocked as Caroline went on. "It's like a bad dream happening all over again!"

Tracy looked confused. "I don't get it. You just said you didn't want Chrissy to feel bad."

"But now I feel left out. I am left out!" Caroline

packed up her uneaten lunch. "Why does everyone have to make such a fuss over poor Chrissy." Even as she said it, Caroline knew she sounded like a crybaby. But she didn't care.

"Chrissy lost her home Cara. That's a terrible thing," Tracy said quietly. "Everyone feels awful for her. We were even thinking of taking up a collection, like a disaster relief fund."

"She's not a charity case!" Caroline's cheeks reddened at the idea.

"It's not an insult," Tracy said. "Okay, we won't do it. I see your point, but we just wanted to help. We all know how much Chrissy was looking forward to her senior year back home."

And I was looking forward to my senior year at Maxwell, Caroline thought, *but nobody cares that it's just gone down the drain.*

"She really wanted to be with her family especially now, to make sure everyone's okay after the tornado."

"My boyfriend was there too," Caroline snapped. "No one's said a thing to me about Luke."

Tracy looked alarmed. "Oh no, Cara—not his house too! Is it gone?"

Caroline looked away, shame-faced. "Uh, actually, no. Just the barn had some damage."

"Oh." Tracy gave her a strange look.

Caroline glanced at her watch. "We'd better go." She scrambled to her feet. "We'll be late for class."

"Well, I'll see you later, huh?"

"Sure. We'll walk home together, maybe."

"Still, it's a great first day of school, isn't it," Tracy said. Caroline could tell she was trying to make up for what she'd done.

"I guess it's going to be a busy year," Caroline said.

"Cara," Tracy said slowly. "I really *am* sorry about what happened."

Caroline couldn't stay mad at her friend for long. Besides, she knew Tracy would never do anything to hurt her on purpose. "Oh well, it isn't the end of the world," she said. "I could always join another committee."

She had tried to sound carefree, and Tracy seemed to believe her—but it wasn't how Caroline felt at all. She really felt awful.

I'm not so selfish, am I? she asked herself as she headed toward her locker. *I'd be really thrilled that Chrissy's back into the swing of things—if only her happiness wasn't at my expense.*

Chapter 4

After school, Tracy was waiting for Caroline at the main doors. "Mad at me?" she asked as soon as she saw Caroline.

Caroline shook her head. "I can't stay mad at you."

"I really didn't mean to hurt your feelings before."

"I know," Caroline assured her. "And I probably overreacted. Sorry, I guess I should be more understanding toward Chrissy."

"Good, because here she comes now."

Chrissy ran up to them. "Wait up, you guys!"

Chrissy's cheeks were bright red and she practically oozed energy. Caroline couldn't help thinking that she certainly didn't look like she'd been through a traumatic experience—in fact, just the opposite.

"You look happy," she commented.

"Big news about the Activities Committee," Chrissy panted.

"No kidding? I never would have guessed," Tracy teased, giving Caroline a conspiratorial grin.

Chrissy blew at the strands of blond hair flopping on her forehead. "Justine and Maria and I went to see Mr. Wells. Know what he said?"

"I think you're about to tell us," Caroline joked, trying to get into the spirit.

Chrissy took a deep breath. "The chairperson isn't an elected position. It's chosen by the senior class president."

"Josh Whooten?"

"Right! And we get along real well. So, Mr. Wells met with Josh and he said he'd be glad to work with me."

"I didn't realize you knew him that well," Caroline said.

"I really don't." Chrissy grinned. "But Josh said he knows me by reputation."

"Who doesn't," Tracy cracked, smiling at Chrissy proudly. "You've got to admit, Chrissy, you've made your mark at Maxwell High."

"And," Chrissy continued, "Josh said he really likes my enthusiasm! Isn't that absolutely wild?"

"Then you're in?" Caroline held her breath.

"Definitely."

Caroline felt a burst of disappointment but ignored it and gave her cousin a big hug.

"I'm glad, Chrissy," she said. "You deserve some good news."

Chrissy's grin was the widest Caroline had ever seen it.

"You really do," Tracy agreed. "You've been through a lot."

A mournful look flashed over Chrissy's face. Caroline thought Chrissy was worrying about her family again, and in that instant, she felt genuinely pleased that Chrissy was chairperson, and not her. But Chrissy's sad expression vanished as quickly as it had come, leaving Caroline wondering if she had been mistaken.

"I can't wait to get started! I've got some great ideas."

"Are you using Cara's suggestions?" Tracy asked.

"Well, um . . . not really. Josh thinks we can come up with better ones," Chrissy remarked.

Caroline stiffened. "I thought my ideas were all right. Some of them, at least. I liked the game show idea."

"Oh, that one's not bad," Chrissy quickly agreed. "But you did say you dashed them off. Josh thinks we can do better if we work at it."

"Of course," Caroline said abruptly. She should have known. Nothing she did was good enough anymore. But she wouldn't complain—that would only make her sound like a bad sport. She'd simply keep quiet and let Chrissy have all the glory.

When they reached the corner where Tracy left them, the girls all said goodbye and waved as Tracy headed up her street. "Congratulations again, Chrissy," she called.

"Thanks!" Gaily, Chrissy skipped a few steps. "Hurry, Cara. I want to get home and tell Aunt Edith and Uncle Richard the good news."

"You go ahead. I can hardly keep up with you."

"Come on, Cara, just move your feet a little faster," Chrissy prodded.

"I don't want to move my feet any faster," Caroline snapped.

"Okay, okay." Chrissy shrugged and waved merrily. "See you, then."

"See you." Alone, Caroline mulled over the day's events.

Am I being a bad sport? she wondered. *Or do I have reason to resent Chrissy? The worst thing is, I can't even ask anyone about it without them thinking I'm terrible. I guess all I can do is pretend I'm not bothered.*

She sighed. It was another one of those times when she had to swallow her own feelings to spare Chrissy's. She just hoped there weren't too many more of them.

Everything was quiet as Caroline let herself in the door to their apartment.

"Mom? Dad? Anybody home?"

"In here, honey."

Caroline followed her father's voice into the corner of the living room where he had his desk set up for work. On the desk to one side of his typewriter lay scattered notecards filled with his illegible scrawl. On the other side a tape recorder played soft classical music. Her mother was there too, and both parents were relaxing with a cup of coffee. Caroline stood by the wide window overlooking the street. "This is a cozy scene," she remarked. "Are you reviewing last night's symphony, Dad?"

He nodded. "Yup. My editor wants three and a half columns by tomorrow."

Caroline gave him a sympathetic smile. "Where's Chrissy?" she asked.

"In your room." Her father grinned. "She is one excited young lady."

"She already told you her news?"

"Yes," her mother answered, "and I'm so glad to see her looking happy. She's hasn't been herself lately."

"She hasn't?" Caroline hadn't noticed Chrissy acting particularly depressed.

"You must know she's been upset about her family."

"Of course I know that. I just don't think she's taking it as hard as everyone else thinks. She seems to have adjusted fine."

"Oh honey, that's just an act," her mother said. "She's acting happy to keep her spirits up. And I know she doesn't want to worry us."

"That's what you think?" Caroline looked at her parents in surprise.

"What else?"

Caroline shrugged. It seemed to her Chrissy had already made a rapid and remarkable recovery. "Nothing. I guess you're right."

Her mother gave her father a sharp look. She drained her coffee. "Well, I've got a portfolio to look over for the gallery. I saw a talented new artist today, and I want to see if her work will fit into our plans for a new exhibit. I'll be in the dining room if you need me."

"And I'd better finish this piece." Her father frowned at his typewriter but didn't make a move to put any paper in.

"I guess I'll go start my homework," Caroline said.

"Wait a minute, hon." Her father looked uncomfortable.

"Is there something wrong, Dad?" *Please*, she thought, *not another pep talk about being nice to Chrissy!*

"How was the first day of school?" he asked.

Caroline shrugged. "Okay, I guess."

"Everything's all right?"

"Of course."

"You're sure?"

"I'm fine," Caroline answered. "Why wouldn't I be? What do I have to complain about?"

Her father seemed satisfied. "Good. Then that's settled." He put a sheet of paper in his typewriter, but Caroline hesitated in the doorway.

"Sweetheart? Is there something else?"

"Actually, there is." Caroline took a deep breath. "I uh, I was wondering. This girl in my old ballet class, do you remember Tais? Well . . . oh, never mind. You wouldn't like the idea."

Her father turned off the typewriter. "What idea?" he asked.

"Well, Tais told me over the summer about this acting class she took. Mostly for poise. But I was thinking, um, maybe that would be good for me, too."

"Acting lessons?" Her father looked surprised. "Isn't this kind of sudden?"

"No. I mean, I've been thinking about it for a long time." Well, that was sort of true, anyway. She'd thought it had sounded interesting when Tais had first told her about the class, but she hadn't considered it seriously for herself until just this afternoon.

"And where would you take these lessons?" her father asked.

"The same place Tais does," Caroline answered. Luckily, she recalled her conversation with her friend in detail. "It's a studio up on Telegraph Hill. Tais says it has a really good reputation. I'd be in the beginners workshop for older teens."

"Sounds like you've researched it."

"I have, Dad," Caroline replied with enthusiasm. She was really warming to the idea. "I have felt sort of aimless since I stopped ballet."

"But you wanted to stop," her father pointed out. "You wanted to spend more time being a 'normal' teenager, as I recall."

"I know," Caroline admitted. "But I guess I'm just the kind of person who needs to be, well, committed to something."

"Yes, I know, and that's a good quality to have, Caroline," her father said. He actually seemed pleased.

"And acting would be good for me," she went on. "It builds self-confidence. So even if I never become a great star or anything, it won't be a waste of time or money." It was a very convincing argument, Caroline thought with satisfaction.

"Time and money." Her father nodded. "Exactly how much of each are we talking about?"

"Only one afternoon a week. And the money isn't much. I could help out more around the house in exchange for it."

Her father smiled. "It sounds like a good opportunity. It's okay with me as long as you get your mother's approval, too."

"I can't believe it! Thanks, Dad. This isn't just a lark, I promise."

"I know, Caroline. I know you. You'll be responsible. But I'd like to know more details."

"I'll find out everything. I'll call right now."

"And it can't interfere with your school work. I don't want your grades to suffer. And," he added, "I don't want you exhausting yourself like you did when you were taking ballet lessons."

"I won't be, Dad," Caroline promised. "I've got tons of energy."

He seemed satisfied. "All right, then. Just don't forget your old dad when you're rich and famous."

"You're the best father in the whole world." Caroline threw her arms around his neck.

"I like to see you happy," he said. "And I think you're talented."

She basked in his unexpected praise. "Thanks, Dad. I won't let you down."

"I know. Now let me get some work done."

Caroline flew down the hall into her room. Chrissy looked up from the desk, obviously startled by her cousin's sudden entrance.

"You look like the cat that swallowed the canary."

"I just got some good news," Caroline said. Grinning broadly, she flopped onto her bed. "My acting class—it's all set. I can hardly believe it!"

"Super." Chrissy chewed on her pencil, distractedly.

Caroline saw that Chrissy had been busy making a list—'Senior Class Activities' was written neatly across a fresh sheet of paper. Several crumpled sheets lay scattered around the floor at Chrissy's feet.

"You're hard at work," Caroline remarked.

"Huh? Oh yeah, I want to get a list together to show Josh tomorrow."

"Don't let me bother you." Caroline dragged the phone into the hall. The acting studio was listed just as she'd remembered it: Bergdorf Studio, with a Telegraph Hill address. She could take a cable car directly there after school. Excitedly, she began to dial, but a moment later she was interupted by the doorbell.

"I'll get it!" She bounded to the door. "Maria! Dino! What are you guys doing here?"

"Inspiration struck." Maria answered, beaming at her boyfriend.

Dino, his hands stuck into his back pockets, rolled his eyes impatiently. "Tell her, already. I've got to get home to dinner."

"You and your stomach." Maria jabbed Dino playfully. "We had the best idea, Cara—let's all go to Mount Tamalpais! We could go this weekend."

Caroline's eyes lit up. "Great! I've been saying we should go there for months. It's been ages since I've climbed to the top."

"Chrissy should love it!" Maria went on. "Let me tell her. This will be a blast."

Caroline's face fell. "Yeah, a blast," she echoed.

Chrissy should love it? I'll love it! Why does everything have to be for Chrissy's sake? You can only take this pity stuff so far, Caroline thought. *Even Chrissy must be getting tired of it by now.*

"It's a great idea," she told Maria dutifully. "Come on up."

Caroline led Maria and Dino up the two flights of

stairs to their third floor apartment.

Dino paused in the doorway to the bedroom. "Wow! This place is even more of a pigsty than my room!"

Caroline flushed, hurriedly stashing a pile of Chrissy's clothes under the bed to make room for her friends to sit down.

"It's not usually such a mess," she apologized.

Chrissy giggled. "Yes, it is. I guess I'm sort of a slob. But Cara puts up with me."

"Lucky me," Caroline mumbled, not meaning anyone to hear. But she caught Maria's look of surprise and resolved to bite her tongue before she made any more sarcastic remarks.

"What's up?" Chrissy asked.

Maria and Dino explained their idea for a trip up Mount Tamalpais.

"As a senior class activity?" Chrissy looked dubious. "Gosh, there's no time to plan it."

"No, just for us," Maria said. "Our group. For fun."

"Oh, Maria! What a great idea!" Chrissy leaped off her chair and danced around the room.

"We'll take Dino's brother's van," Maria continued, "and bring a picnic."

"That will be wonderful!" Chrissy exclaimed. "I can't wait 'til Saturday! You know, back in Iowa, we don't have many mountains to climb."

Caroline saw Maria and Dino exchange a look that clearly said "Poor Chrissy".

"Um, this does sound terrific, count me in," Caroline told them, "but I have to make an important phone call. If you don't mind?"

"We don't mind," Chrissy said, hugging her arms

in excitement. "Don't worry, Cara, we'll settle the details."

"Sure. Go make your call," Maria nodded.

"Okay. I'll be done in a minute."

But by the time she had finished getting all the information from the receptionist at the acting school, Maria and Dino were already heading down the stairs, calling goodbyes. With mixed feelings, Caroline watched them go. She knew the trip would be lots of fun, but she wasn't looking forward to it as much as she should have been. *There's no reason for me to feel left out,* she thought. *So why do I?*

Chapter 5

On Saturday morning, however, Caroline did wake with a feeling of anticipation. "Chrissy," she called, rolling out of bed. "Time to get up."

Chrissy grunted.

"Come on—we can't be late." Caroline stumbled down the hall into the bathroom. It was terrible to wake up early on a Saturday, but getting an early start up Mount Tamalpais would make it worthwhile. There was almost nothing she loved better than the spectacular view from the mountaintop. All of Marin County was spread out below, with a vista of over a hundred miles in every direction.

"It's worth losing a little sleep for that," she thought, as she scrubbed her teeth.

By the time she was dressed Chrissy still hadn't stirred. "Chrissy," she urged, shaking her cousin lightly, "better hurry. We're supposed to be ready by eight, and you said you wanted time to call home before we leave."

"Hmm?" Chrissy pushed herself onto her elbows to stare bleary-eyed at Caroline. "What time is it?"

"Nearly quarter to. They'll be here any minute. Look, I'll take our sweaters and stuff in my knapsack. If I make lunch, will you carry it?"

"Sure. Leave it on the kitchen counter for me."

"Okay, but get up! We'll miss the whole trip."

Leaving Chrissy to rouse herself, Caroline hurried to the kitchen. She and Chrissy were assigned the desserts, and she had stayed up late, making her specialty: extra-rich brownies. The secret was in the Dutch cocoa powder she used instead of regular cooking chocolate. It was worth the work to think of the pleasure her friends always got from the brownies. Not to mention their praise!

At the last minute, she added a field snack of nuts and raisins. The snack would be good for extra energy, and they might need it. She was sure they'd choose the difficult path today. All of them, except Chrissy, had climbed Mount Tamalpais several times before, so the gentle path was no challenge at all.

Leaving the food neatly packed on the counter along with the canteens full of water, where Chrissy would be sure to see everything, she flung her knapsack over her shoulder and hurried downstairs to wait on the front porch.

In no time, Dino's brother's van appeared. Caroline waved and leaped down to meet them. "Great day, isn't it?"

Maria, perched beside Dino on the driver's seat, stared as if Caroline were crazy.

"Fog is great?" The valley where the street dipped down was lost in a pocket of thick fog. Mist wafted down the sidewalk alongside.

"It will be great when this burns off," Caroline grinned.

Dino climbed in back to stash Caroline's gear.

"I hope you got your beauty sleep," Justine teased.

"I hope I got my *energy* sleep," Caroline joked back.

The boy sitting next to Justine gave her a mischievous grin. "Did *you* get your beauty sleep, Justine?"

Justine tossed her head smartly, her blond hair falling perfectly back into place. "As a matter of fact, Randy," she told him, "I don't even need any beauty sleep."

Everyone in the van groaned good-naturedly and Justine laughed along with the others.

Caroline took her place beside Tracy, shooting her a friendly smile. Dino had flipped down the extra passenger seat in the back to make space for everyone. With Dino and Maria, Justine and Randy, Tracy, Caroline, and Chrissy, they needed all the space they could get.

"Where's Chrissy?" Tracy asked.

"She overslept. She also wanted to call her family before we left."

Maria turned from the front seat. "How is her family? How are they all taking it?"

"They're not too happy," Caroline admitted. "It's been especially hard on Chrissy's father. He can't work his land or anything. They're still waiting to see if they'll get insurance money."

"At least they don't have to worry about Chrissy," Maria said.

"That's right," Justine agreed. "Chrissy's doing the right thing, staying with you. It makes it easier on her folks."

"It wasn't exactly her choice," Caroline answered, recalling Chrissy's reaction when she realized she would have to stay in San Francisco.

"Still, it's one less mouth they have to feed," Randy commented.

"And one less worry," Maria added. "At least they know Chrissy will be clothed and fed. It was good of your family to take her in," she told Caroline.

"It's not like that either," Caroline said uncomfortably. "I mean, we don't think of it as a big favor or anything. Chrissy is family."

"Well, I say she's very sensible, staying here," Justine said.

"She's also pretty late," Dino complained. "Cara— can you hurry her up?"

Maria punched him lightly in the arm. "Give Chrissy a break. She's talking to her family."

"Hey, she can talk to *my* family anytime," Dino said, "and I won't charge long distance."

"And your house won't have to be blown away by a tornado either," Randy added.

"Not very funny," Tracy told him. Even Justine gave him a sharp look.

"Seriously," Dino pleaded, "I thought we wanted to get started before the tourists descend."

"Dino's right," Maria agreed. "If we want the trail to ourselves, we've got to leave now. That was the whole point of leaving so early."

Caroline slid off her seat. "I'll see if I can hurry her along."

She took the front porch steps two at a time and climbed the two flights up to their apartment. *I'll be exhausted from this before we even get to the mountain,* she thought wryly.

Chrissy was on the phone in the hallway, her knapsack and a paper bag lying at her feet. Caroline motioned that she'd carry the things down for her. Chrissy nodded okay. "Hurry," Caroline mouthed.

Climbing back down the stairs, Caroline couldn't help thinking that Chrissy seemed fine. She wasn't at all upset like she had been at first. Maybe things were going better for them. That would be a relief, anyway.

"Well? Where is she?" Dino had already started the engine.

"She's coming." Caroline dumped Chrissy's things in the back. "It's getting crowded in here," she said, attempting to lighten things up. She could tell Dino and Randy were pretty impatient, if not the girls. And naturally, Caroline felt responsible. Yet, what could she do? *I'm only Chrissy's cousin, not her mother,* she thought as she settled into her seat.

By the time a few more minutes went by, Dino and Randy were really grumbling. Justine seemed impatient too, although Maria and Tracy were nice about it. "There's plenty of time," Tracy kept saying. "The mountain's not going anywhere."

Finally Chrissy appeared. "It's about time," Dino grumbled.

Maria gave him a dirty look. "How's everything

at home? Is your family okay?" she asked in concern.

"Yeah, are they eating your uncle out of house and barn?" Randy joked.

"All you think about is food," Justine complained.

Chrissy grinned good-naturedly as she plopped down into the extra passenger seat. "They're just fine," she said brightly. "The boys are really impressed that I'm climbing a mountain with three-hundred-foot-high trees today."

"I guess that is pretty impressive," Maria said thoughtfully. "I take it for granted."

"It's hard to take a mountain for granted when all you've ever seen is farmland as flat as a checkerboard," Chrissy pointed out.

"I've lived here all my life and I still think the giant redwoods are amazing," Tracy remarked.

"Well, if I live here for the rest of my life, I'll never take the redwoods for granted," Chrissy said cheerfully. "No way."

Caroline felt a jolt of fear. *The rest of her life? Chrissy doesn't mean that. I know she doesn't mean it.*

Still, the thought left Caroline so shaken, she could hardly show enthusiasm for the gorgeous scenery, not even when they drove across the Golden Gate Bridge, one of her favorite sites in the Bay area.

When they arrived at the base of the mountain, Dino left the van in a shady spot in the parking lot. Everyone grabbed their knapsacks. "Hold on," Randy said. "I want to fill my canteen."

"Me too," Maria said. "Thanks for reminding me.

I'd be pretty miserable up there without enough water."

Chrissy gulped, looking at Caroline strangely. "Were . . . were we supposed to bring canteens?"

"Of course." Caroline gaped at her. "You didn't leave them, did you? Chrissy, we can't climb with no water!"

"Sorry, Caroline, I didn't realize . . ."

"Hey, it's okay," Randy cut in. "I've got a thermos in the van. You can use that."

"That's a relief," Caroline said. "Well, at least we have the dessert. I hope you're all ready for my special brownies."

"Special brownies?" There was a strange look on Chrissy's face.

"The ones I made last night. They're in the paper bag."

"Oh Cara, I'm so glad you remembered that bag on the counter," Chrissy said, sighing with relief. "I completely forgot."

A warning bell rang in Caroline's head. "You mean you didn't even touch the bag on the counter?" she asked. Chrissy shook her head. "Then I took the wrong paper bag!" Caroline flung off her knapsack and threw the bag open. "Oh no! What are these?" Groaning, she lifted a pair of shoes in the air.

"Old shoes?" Randy was aghast. "You forgot the brownies and brought shoes?"

"We're supposed to eat shoes for dessert?" Maria looked disappointed.

"Oh, great," Justine snapped. "Count on you to do one little thing."

Caroline flushed hotly. "It was an accident. A mistake."

"I'll say," Randy groaned.

Chrissy frowned. "Why'd you bring that bag, Cara?"

"It was in the hall, by the telephone. I thought you had taken the bag from the counter and put it by the phone so you wouldn't forget it. I made a perfect batch of brownies, and a field snack too," she added sadly.

"I had my heart set on those brownies," Tracy mused. "Too bad."

Chrissy looked at Caroline like she was crazy. "That bag was for the shoe repair shop. Your mother left it in the hall so she wouldn't forget it this morning."

"But I thought it was the bag of food from the kitchen," Caroline repeated in exasperation. "You were supposed to carry the food, remember?"

Chrissy smiled weakly. "I was so excited about talking to my family, I guess I forgot. I never went in the kitchen this morning. I'm sorry."

"Oh, that's okay, Chrissy," Maria said. "You were upset about your house and all."

"Who needs brownies anyway," Tracy chimed in. "Too fattening."

"Especially the way Cara makes them," Randy joked, "with all that extra chocolate."

"And sweets don't really give you energy," Justine said reasonably. "We're better off without them."

"Don't worry about it," Tracy said warmly. The others agreed.

Chrissy sighed. "I'm really sorry, guys."

"No problem." Randy clapped her on the shoulder. "Just excess baggage."

They began getting ready to climb. Caroline took Chrissy aside. "I don't believe this! You promised to take the dessert. I left everything on the counter where you'd be sure to see it."

"No one minds," Chrissy said, "so it's no big deal, is it?"

I mind, Caroline thought angrily, but instead she just said, "It would have been nice to have those brownies for dessert, that's all."

"Take it easy, Cara," Maria said. "It really wasn't her fault. She had a lot on her mind."

Caroline opened her mouth to reply, but thought better of it. "I guess so," she muttered.

"I have some fruit we can all share," Tracy said hurriedly. "We've got enough without dessert, don't we, guys?"

"Sure we do," Justine said, looping an arm around Chrissy's shoulder. "Poor Chrissy. It's not a big deal."

"No use crying over spilt milk," Chrissy said brightly.

Caroline was so disappointed she felt like screaming, but what was the point? Chrissy was right. There was no use complaining. It wouldn't get the brownies back.

They did take the difficult trail, with Randy and Dino in the lead. Tracy, Maria, and Chrissy followed with Caroline taking the rear. She was glad to be left alone. Her bad mood was quickly fading as she concentrated on finding safe footholds. Soon she had forgotten everything. She was absorbed in the rhythm of the climb, the soothing scent of the trees, and the scrunch of pine needles underfoot. Over-head, the branches of the giant redwoods formed a cool, green canopy. The higher they climbed, the better Caroline felt.

The gang stopped to rest at the lookout point that Caroline loved. Her idea of paradise was to sit there quietly, with the magnificent view of the forest spread out below.

"Let's eat," Chrissy said loudly. "I'm starved."

"It's early," Caroline said sensibly. "We should snack now and save lunch for the top of the mountain."

"If I don't eat, I won't make it to the top," Chrissy said.

"I could eat," Randy announced.

"So what else is new?" Justine rolled her eyes.

Tracy and Maria hesitated. "I guess I could eat something," Tracy finally said. Maria opened her knapsack and took out the bag of sandwiches.

Giving in, Caroline sat too. "Okay, what do we get?"

Everyone dug into Maria's bag and came up with an odd assortment of sandwiches, including liver-wurst, which was Randy's favorite, tuna, and sev-eral squashed and leaky peanut butter and jellies. Caroline longed for the tasty lunch sitting at home on the kitchen counter, but she had to admit, it could have been worse.

"We really made good time," Maria said.

"We sure did." Caroline inhaled deeply, stretching her arms luxuriously over her head. There was just enough sun to warm her without being in the least hot—a perfect day! "Isn't this gorgeous?"

"It is pretty spectacular," Tracy mused, sitting quietly beside Caroline.

"I know!" Chrissy jumped up excitedly. "Let's have a sing-a-long!"

Caroline looked up, startled. "But it's so peaceful and quiet here."

"Exactly. Let's shake it up a little," Chrissy enthused.

"You mean, like around a campfire?" Justine looked doubtful.

Randy and Dino groaned. "Give me a break," Dino muttered.

"It'll be loads of fun. We'll do a round. Come on, pretend we're not sophisticated seniors. It'll be fun."

Caroline could hardly believe it, but in a few minutes Chrissy had them singing rounds—old camp songs, and songs she hadn't sung since grade school. Even Justine was acting like she enjoyed it.

They all feel so sorry for Chrissy that they'll do anything! Caroline thought.

Chrissy glanced at her cousin. "Smile, Cara! You look as sour as a pail of rotten apples."

Caroline forced a smile to her lips. Beside her, Tracy grinned in amusement, then squeezed her hand. "Good for you," she whispered when Chrissy wasn't looking. "I think Chrissy's being very brave. I bet nothing ever fazes her."

"Hardly anything," Caroline had to agree.

"She's been through a lot," Tracy continued, "but I think we're making her really happy."

Caroline smiled sweetly. "That's all that matters, isn't it?"

In the center of their circle, Chrissy was all smiles, eagerly leading the singing. If anything,

Caroline thought, she was more cheerful than ever.

Caroline gritted her teeth. "Let's sing another one," she said with false enthusiasm.

Tracy patted her approvingly on the back. "That's the spirit. Let's sing some more."

Chapter 6

Caroline took a deep breath. The door to the Bergdorf Acting Studio loomed before her, larger than life. She was almost afraid to go in. Had she made a mistake? After all, it had been a whim to come here—a spur of the moment idea.

On the other hand, she loved being onstage. Dancing had been the highpoint of her life. Although she'd hated the hard work, and especially her bully of a dance teacher, she had loved the audience's attention and their applause.

Acting would be just as exciting, and hopefully not as much work. She'd really be able to shine as an actress, Caroline thought. She would always have her own part to play. It might be a very small part, but it would be hers alone. It would be like having a dance solo, over and over again. Part of her loved that idea.

And part of me is scared out of my wits.

As she stood there, wavering between going inside and running away, a boy came and stood by the doorway. He took out a piece of paper and looked at the number over the door, checking it against the piece of paper. He looked about Caroline's age. He wasn't much taller than she, with a slight build, and he had a nice face, she noticed, with curly brown hair and light blue eyes.

"Um, excuse me," she said. "This is the Bergdorf Studio, if that's what you're looking for."

He nearly jumped when she spoke to him.

"Sorry," she apologized. "I didn't mean to startle you."

"Oh, I, uh, that's okay," he said nervously. "I guess I was so busy checking the address I didn't notice you." He smiled and suddenly he looked like a devilish little boy. "Are you going in?"

Caroline put on a confident air. "Yes. I'm starting acting lessons today. Just a beginner's workshop."

"Me too!" He looked enormously relieved. "It sounds great, doesn't it? The brochure really made me want to sign up in a hurry."

"I didn't see the brochure," Caroline explained. "But I'd heard this place was good, so I registered over the phone."

"Just like that?" He gave her an admiring glance. "I've been thinking about this for years. Finally, I told myself I had to come." He took the crumpled brochure from his pocket and smoothed it out.

"Can I see that?" Caroline inspected the dog-eared brochure. "Sounds impressive. And like a lot of work."

"That doesn't bother me," the boy said. "I'd do anything to be an actor."

"I don't really mind the work too much. It's just that . . ." Caroline hesitated. She didn't usually talk so freely to strangers. "Well, I used to do some dancing. It got pretty demanding and I decided to drop out. I didn't want my whole life to be about thin thighs and muscle tone."

"Sounds like you were pretty serious."

"I was. Anyway, I imagined acting classes would be more fun. But this sounds just as hard."

"That's okay. It has to be hard to teach you anything."

Impulsively, Caroline held out her hand. "I'm Caroline Kirby," she said.

"I'm Zach Landau. And you have a great name. Did you change it?"

Caroline laughed heartily. "No. I never even thought of that. What about yours?"

"Mine's real too. It's a pretty good name for an actor, but it wasn't real easy to grow up with. Zachary Landau." He made a face.

"I like it," Caroline protested. "It has a nice ring to it: Starring Zachary Landau. Very distinctive."

Zach's face lit up. "Thanks. You know, I have a confession to make."

"What?"

"Well—I'm pretty nervous. I've never done anything like this before. I'm not an experienced performer, like you."

"I know about first-night jitters," Caroline admitted, "but I don't think that will help my acting." She smiled, trying to put Zach at his ease. He kept glancing at the door, looking the way she felt—like he wanted to run away.

Nervously, Zach pushed his hair behind his ears.

"But I never even had a part in a school play."

"Did you ever audition?"

"No," he confessed. "There was no point. The good parts always went to the popular kids." He shrugged.

"I know how that is," Caroline assured him. "But I wouldn't let that discourage you."

"You wouldn't?"

"School has nothing to do with being a professional." She frowned, thinking it through. "I danced in a school musical once, but that was nothing like real ballet."

"Really?"

"Not a bit."

"Well, how did you know that you could dance ballet in the first place?" asked Zach.

"I just knew," Caroline replied with a shrug.

Zach nodded. "That's how I feel about acting. Something in me says I can do it." He gave her another admiring glance. "You sure have a lot of confidence."

Caroline blinked in surprise. "That's funny. I don't think of myself that way."

Other people were going into the studio as she and Zach talked. Most of them looked a lot older than they, even though the brochure specified older teens. For the first time, Caroline realized that could mean college students of eighteen and nineteen. She felt nervous all over again.

Zach seemed to be thinking along the same lines. "What if *everyone* has lots of experience?" He looked pretty worried. "Maybe I shouldn't be here at all."

"Don't say that," Caroline snapped. She had

sounded so harsh she was surprised and laughed at herself. "I'm sure it's fine. After all, if they knew everything about acting they wouldn't be in the beginner's class, right?"

"Right." Zach smiled back gratefully. He squared his shoulders. "Let's go in together, okay? Before I lose my nerve."

"Sure."

Caroline was glad to have someone to walk into the classroom with. Everyone in the room seemed to examine them as they entered. She told herself they were probably as nervous as she and Zach, but she didn't really believe it.

Stay calm. You don't have to perform yet. she told herself.

The workshop leader, Loretta Forest, came in and introduced herself. She was a tall woman, in her early thirties, with beautiful, dark, wavy hair that nearly reached her waist. She recited a long list of credits, including guest spots on some popular TV shows. Caroline thought she recognized her from a perfume commercial, but she couldn't be sure.

Loretta had them sit in a big circle. "I'll tell you a bit more about what we'll be doing in the next few weeks. Now is the time to ask all your questions." Immediately, a half-dozen hands shot up. Loretta laughed. "Not a shy bunch—good. After the questions, we'll choose up partners for some beginning exercises."

"Exercises?" One of the girls frowned.

"Movement and relaxation techniques are an important part of acting," Loretta told her. "Every actor or actress has to use their whole body. But don't worry, I'm not talking about sit-ups and push-ups. You'll see what I mean."

Beside her, Caroline saw Zach push his hair behind his ears again. Impulsively, she leaned over. "Zach—be my partner, okay? These exercises sound intimidating."

He looked relieved. "Sure. No problem, Caroline."

Caroline hesitated. "Call me Cara. Everyone does."

"Okay Cara," Zach whispered, then put his index finger to his lips, signaling Caroline that he wanted to listen to the class.

Caroline smiled at him in understanding, then turned her attention back to Loretta's description of the class. She was glad she'd run into Zachary. He seemed really nice. Plus, she realized, she had been so busy reassuring him that she'd forgotten about her own butterflies!

Acting lessons are good for me. I'm feeling more confident already!

Cara checked her watch for the tenth time. Where was Chrissy, anyway? Her first official senior coffee hour was supposed to start in ten minutes, and still no sign of her. The classroom they'd been assigned was ready. All the desks had been pushed aside and Caroline had taken it upon herself to arrange the chairs in casual groups to encourage conversation. She'd also dragged a long table to the front of the room for the refreshments. Someone had left an electric coffee pot for them, and she'd already filled it with clean water and plugged it in to preheat.

But now she needed the coffee to put in it. Unfortunately, Chrissy had the coffee, and everything else they needed. Just then, footsteps sounded in the hall and a second later Chrissy burst into the room, loaded down with parcels.

"Chrissy! Where've you been?"

"Golly, Caroline, I almost didn't make it at all! I got stuck in the donut shop." With an exasperated sigh, Chrissy dumped her things on the table. She had bags of Styrofoam cups, two cans of coffee, and boxes of fresh donuts. "Thank goodness you started without me."

"Someone had to. You're awfully late."

"I know. Thanks for coming—I could never get through this alone."

"Well, I said I'd help."

"Gosh—there's no time to set up, people will be here any minute!" Hurriedly, Chrissy opened the coffee and dumped some into a clean filter. She started to arrange the cups and packets of cream and sugar on the table. She picked up the donut boxes. "I know," she said, stacking the boxes under the table, "I'll leave the refreshments 'til last—that way, people will have to stay, if they want anything to eat."

"But if you don't feed them, they might leave early," Caroline pointed out.

Chrissy's hand hovered in mid-air. "Gosh, do you think so?" She frowned, then brightened. "I'll ply them with food first," she declared. "They'll be happy and they'll volunteer more."

"Good idea," Cara said politely. Lately, it seemed like Chrissy was taking all her ideas without giving her one ounce of credit. She was getting pretty tired of it.

Chrissy pulled the donut boxes out. "Hmmm.

Cara, you're the artistic type. Do something with this table, will you?" She stepped back, as if studying the table. "The food should look really appetizing."

"Where are all your committee members?" Cara asked. "Shouldn't they help you?"

"Oh, they'll be here in plenty of time," Chrissy assured her. "Just help me get started. Please?"

It was hard to resist Chrissy's pleading look. "Okay. I'll do the best I can." Carefully, Cara set out neat stacks of cups and plastic spoons. She arranged the donuts in attractive pyramids on paper plates. By the time she was done, people were starting to gather in the room.

"What will you do first," Caroline asked.

"First?" Chrissy shrugged. "Say hello to everyone. This is casual, just a coffee hour."

Caroline rolled her eyes. "Chrissy, you need a plan. Or is everyone just going to eat donuts all day?"

Chrissy looked at her blankly. "I don't know. I guess I thought things would sort of run themselves. I thought we'd eat and talk at the same time."

"That's no way to run things." Caroline pulled a notebook out of her purse. "I think you should welcome everyone first, so they know what this coffee hour is for. Then ask for suggestions and take notes."

Chrissy nodded. "Okay."

Justine and Randy entered with a group of seniors Caroline hardly knew. Chrissy flew to them, laughing and exchanging gossip. More and more people came in, but Chrissy was so involved in her

conversation, she didn't seem to notice. Caroline
saw some kids taking donuts and leaving the room.
Caroline plowed through the crowd and tugged at
Chrissy's sleeve.

"I think you'd better start," she said. "You'll be out
of food before the meeting gets going."

Chrissy smiled at her. "But everyone's having a
good time. I don't want to break things up yet. If
they're happy, the meeting will go much better."

Caroline gave her a skeptical look.

"Please, Cara—let's do it my way."

Caroline made her way to the few people she
knew who were hanging on the edge of the crowd.
If she couldn't be leading the committee, she could
still help in an unofficial capacity. She could drum
up enthusiasm for Chrissy's ideas.

But Caroline had barely started saying hello
when Chrissy decided to get started. She strode to
the front of the room, clapping her hands for
attention.

"Hi everyone! For all those who don't know me,
I'm Chrissy Madden, this year's Chairman—Chairperson—of the Senior Activities Committee."

There was scattered applause. Justine and Randy
cheered good-naturedly.

"Did you all have something to eat? I want
everyone to help themselves to refreshments. Then
I'm going to outline my plans for the year."

Caroline felt a tingle of excitement. She had a
couple more ideas she hadn't told Chrissy yet. She
could hardly wait to suggest them.

There was a dash to the table for the last donuts.
Randy helped himself to a cup of coffee.

"Yecch!" Unceremoniously, he spit the coffee

back into his cup. "Call this coffee?"

"Tastes more like mud!" someone called from the back of the room. Everyone else nodded in agreement and began talking among themselves about the terrible coffee.

Anxiously, Chrissy poured herself a cup. She tasted it gingerly. Her expression showed she didn't like it any better than Randy did. She motioned to Caroline, who hurried to the refreshment table.

"What's wrong with this coffee?" Chrissy asked. "It's disgusting."

Cara picked up the coffee can. "Chrissy," she hissed, "this is espresso drip. It's very strong and it's definitely not for percolators."

"Oh no," Chrissy moaned. "Cara, help! We need something decent to drink."

"What do you want me to do?"

"Get the right coffee?"

"You want me to go to the store now?" Caroline put the coffee can back on the table with a thud.

"You have to," Chrissy said. "This could ruin my whole meeting."

"Can't someone else go?"

"Like who?"

"Like one of your committee members."

"I can't ask them to do this! I need to keep their enthusiasm high. If I send them to the store first thing, they'll get turned off. Come on, Cara. Pretty please?" Chrissy gazed at Caroline with pleading eyes.

Unfortunately, Caroline could see some logic in what Chrissy said. "Okay, I'll go. But just this once."

"And get some more donuts. We're running out," Chrissy added, pulling an envelope out of her

pocket. She slipped a five-dollar bill from the
envelope and gave it to Caroline.

Naturally, the lines in the store were unbelievable. Caroline stewed. This was hardly her idea of
contributing to the Activities Committee. But she
told herself to be calm. She could still help with her
suggestions. She had a fabulous idea for Senior Skit
Night. Her acting class had inspired her to create a
whole new role for the Master of Ceremonies. It
was brilliant! Never for one minute did she doubt
that it was the perfect job for her.

Finally, she got through the line and paid for
everything. Hurrying as fast as she could, she made
it back to school in record time. Ideas were spin-
ning through her head, one after the other. She had
a whole year's worth of activities planned by the
time she reached the classroom.

"What's happening?"

A group of sophomores were gathered outside,
blocking the door.

"You should hear this," a perky redhead told her.
"That's the girl whose house was blown away in the
tornado. It's incredible!"

Pushing past, Caroline could hear murmurs of
disbelief greeting Chrissy's vivid description of a
tornado slicing across farmland.

"The sky gets completely still," Chrissy was saying in a dramatic voice, "the color of . . . of gray
slate." She paused, and her audience stopped talking so they could pay full attention to Chrissy.
"Everything gets dead silent. The animals know
first. There's an instant of warning, and then
BOOM!" She clapped her hands together. Several
kids jumped. "Disaster!"

Chrissy finished speaking to more murmurs of sympathy and disbelief. Caroline set her parcels down on a desk while the talk swirled around her.

"Imagine that," someone said. "She's so lucky she was here."

"She would have been killed if she had been doing her barn chores," her friend agreed.

Barn chores? Caroline couldn't believe it. Instead of discussing the senior treasury, Chrissy had them all enthralled with tales of farm life!

"Look at the time," Chrissy suddenly cried. "We're supposed to clear out at four-thirty. Meeting adjourned."

Cara was astounded. Kids poured out of the room. She grabbed Chrissy. "I just got back and you adjourn the meeting?"

"Cara! Where were you? What took so long?"

Caroline gaped at her. "For one thing, the lines were long, and the checkout lady ran out of change. Plus you didn't give me enough money and I had to use my own. And now there's no meeting." She thrust the grocery bag at Chrissy. "Here. Take your groceries."

Chrissy set the bag down, sputtering. "For gosh sake's, Cara, if you'd been here on time, there would be a meeting."

"It's *my* fault?" Caroline stared, astonished.

"You're the one who said to keep kids happy. They had nothing to drink, so I was forced to tell these long stories to keep them entertained."

"You love telling those stories. I've heard them a million times. No one can *stop* you from telling them!"

Stubbornly, Chrissy crossed her arms. "They

asked me about it. Anyway, it's done."

"As long as you formed a committee, I guess it doesn't matter," Caroline said.

"But I never had a chance to go over activities," Chrissy complained. "You heard—we have to clean up at four-thirty." She jerked the percolator cord out of the wall and began stacking the unused paper plates.

"You didn't get anything done?"

"How could I? I didn't have a chance." Chrissy glared at Caroline.

"Don't act like it's my fault," Caroline warned.

"You're the one late with the coffee."

"You're the one who got the wrong thing to begin with."

"Well, how was I supposed to know?" Chrissy shouted.

"I don't know," Caroline snapped, "but that's your problem. You're the chairperson of the Activities Committee, remember?"

"So, you're my cousin. You're supposed to help me out," Chrissy retorted.

They stared at each other. Neither of them wanted to back down. In silence, Chrissy threw away the trash and began to drag the desks back in place.

"What are you going to do," Caroline asked finally.

Chrissy shrugged. "We'll have another coffee hour. Say, day after tomorrow?"

"Don't look at me. I can't be here then."

"You said you'd help!" Chrissy protested.

Caroline shook her head in disbelief. "I said I'd help today! I'm rehearsing with my friend Zach the day after tomorrow. We've got an assignment for acting class."

Chrissy looked hurt. "Can't you postpone it? I thought you wanted to help. You said you cared about the committee."

Caroline threw her hands up in exasperation. "I do care. I did want to help. Chrissy, I tried!"

"You're not trying very hard if you won't come to the meetings," Chrissy declared.

Caroline felt helpless. "I give up, Chrissy. You just don't get it. From now on, count me out of this committee."

"Boy, Caroline. I never thought you'd be a quitter."

"I'm not. I—oh, forget it." Caroline didn't have the strength to explain. "Sometimes, Chrissy, you push me too far."

"That's all you have to say?"

Caroline nodded.

"I'm surprised at you," Chrissy said quietly. "I feel like you're deserting me."

"Don't be so dramatic, Chrissy. I'm the one taking acting classes, remember?"

"Well," Chrissy said, "we have to make our own choices in life. That's what my mom always says. I guess you've made yours."

Or maybe you made it for me, Caroline thought, storming toward the door.

"I don't see what you've got to be angry about," Chrissy called after her.

"No, of course you don't," Caroline muttered. "Nobody does but me."

Chapter 7

"We have the dining room to ourselves," Caroline told Zach as he followed her down the long hall. It was the Friday after their first acting class, and Caroline was looking forward to their rehearsal. She and Chrissy had barely been speaking all week, and she was glad to have something else to think about.

"This is a nice apartment," Zach said. "I hope we won't be bothering anyone," he added, although there was no one in sight except Caroline.

"Don't worry. My dad is working in the living room, but nobody else is home," Caroline answered.

Zach heaved a sigh of relief. "Oh good. I didn't want anyone to hear us rehearsing. The only audience I'm used to is my own reflection in the mirror." He laughed awkwardly.

Caroline hid her smile. Zach was so sweet, and so ridiculously unsure of himself. He'd certainly have to stop being so self-conscious if he wanted to be an actor.

"Well, my dad said not to disturb him right now, anyway, but I'll introduce you later."

"That's okay," Zach said. "I don't want to be a bother."

"You're not a bother." Caroline shook her head. "Do you have your copy of the scene?"

Loretta had assigned each set of partners one short scene that was supposed to help them stretch their imaginations.

"Okay," Caroline said brusquely. "First time through, I play the girl's part and you play the boy's."

"That's right," Zach agreed. "But then we switch places. You play the boy, I play the girl."

Caroline sighed. "I still don't see how we can take that seriously. It's silly."

"It does sound silly," Zach agreed, "but Loretta said not to make judgments. Let's try it and see."

They went over their lines a few times, and then Zach suggested they do the scene with more feeling. He began acting it out, glancing at the script every now and then.

"Is something wrong?" Zach stopped reading. Caroline was watching him with her mouth open.

"Wrong? No! I mean, you're really good," she blurted out. "It's like . . . the scene is *real* when you say the lines."

Zach ducked his head in embarrassment. "Thanks. But I've got lots more work to do on it. This is only the beginning."

"If you're at the beginning," Caroline asked, "where am I? I can't act that well."

Zach beamed. "Sure you can. Just put your whole self into it."

They continued with the scene and Zach's reading was so alive that Caroline found herself drawn into the part of her own character. She'd practiced the lines dozens of times in front of her own mirror, but had never felt anything like this. Zach was so natural, she forgot herself completely.

"That was absolutely fantastic!" she cried when they finished. "You really sounded angry, as if you believed it was *me* who was two-timing you, and not just some character in a play. You even made me act my part better."

"Maybe I should be an acting coach," Zach suggested.

"Maybe you should be an actor," Caroline told him.

Zach smiled. "Wait 'til we're finished to decide. Now let's switch parts. You're the boy, I'm the girl."

"Okay, but I really doubt that I can act like the boy in this scene."

"Stretch your imagination," Zach instructed. "Let's go."

Caroline struck a pose and began the scene.

"Whoa," Zach suddenly stopped her. "What are you doing?"

"Being the boy. I'm acting angry. Isn't he supposed to be angry?"

"Angry? You sound like you're going to jump off a bridge."

Caroline flushed with embarrassment. "Oh. I—I thought I was doing it the way you did."

Zach nodded thoughtfully. "That's the problem. You can't copy me."

"I guess I thought your . . . interpretation . . . was right."

"Right for me, not for you." Zach turned the script back a few pages. "Start here, and be yourself."

"How can I be myself when I'm acting the part of a boy?"

Zach grinned. "I mean, find your own answer. Don't copy me being the boy."

"I'll try." Clearing her throat, Caroline began to read self-consciously. *Maybe this is a big mistake. I'm no actress!*

"Hold it, Cara." Again Zach interrupted, putting a hand to his forehead.

"But I was trying not to imitate you," Caroline said, completely baffled. She thought she'd done much better that time.

"Yes, but it still doesn't sound realistic. I mean, I know I'm no expert, but something's wrong," Zach said.

"Maybe I'm no actress." Discouraged, Caroline sank onto a chair.

"That's not it." Zach pulled out a chair and faced her. "I know. Why don't we just read through the dialogue? You be the boy and I'll be the girl, but we won't act it out, we'll just read the scene straight, so it becomes more natural." He looked at her patiently. "What do you say?"

Caroline shrugged. "It's worth a try."

"Good." Zach smiled. "You start."

Caroline looked down at her script and took a deep breath. "I saw you at the park last night, Gloria," she began.

"So?" Zach replied.

"With Ralph," she added.

"Oh," Zach said. "What were you doing there?"

"I was walking the dog." Caroline paused. "What about you and Ralph?"

"Well, we were just admiring the lovely flowers."

"Don't try to fool me," Caroline said. "You act so innocent, but that's all it is—an act. Maybe you can fool everyone else, but I've caught onto your little tricks now." As she spoke, Caroline's voice became harsher, and this time her anger sounded very realistic. "I thought I could trust you," she went on, "but now I know better. You don't care about me, all you care about is—"

"Whoa, Cara. Take it easy." Zach reached over and gave her shoulder a gentle shake. "We were just going to read the dialogue this time, without acting it out. Remember?"

"Oh yeah," Caroline said. "Sorry."

Zach studied her curiously. "Is something wrong?" he asked. "You sounded like you were talking to a real person, and it wasn't Gloria."

"Sorry," Caroline apologized again. "I didn't realize it was that obvious." She paused, looking at his friendly blue eyes. "I don't know where to start."

"How about at the beginning?"

"The beginning is how my cousin Chrissy came to live with me," she began. Caroline told him everything; all about their adventures and misadventures, mixing the good in with the bad.

"It took a year," she explained, "but Chrissy and I really learned to love each other for our differences. And then . . ."

Zach's eyes widened with interest. "And then," he prompted.

Caroline turned her head away. Haltingly, she described the shocking news of the tornado that had demolished Chrissy's home, and how the Maddens thought Chrissy should stay with the Kirbys another full year.

"But that's not the worst," Caroline continued. "The worst is that I had wanted so badly to be a real part of my class this year." She told him how Chrissy had gotten the job of Activities Chairperson instead of her, and how the first meeting had been a disaster.

"I hate to admit it, but I think I'm jealous of Chrissy," she finished.

"Let me get this straight," Zach said, serious now. "Your cousin came to stay for a year and now because of a tornado, she's staying for another year?"

"That's right."

Zach shook his head. "Truth is stranger than fiction."

"You're right," Caroline said, "but I don't know what to do about it. The more people feel sorry for Chrissy the angrier I seem to get." She hesitated. "I guess I'm a pretty horrible person."

"I think you've got a legitimate gripe."

"You think so?"

"Sure. You must feel squeezed out."

Caroline nodded thoughtfully. "It's just that Chrissy has this great tragedy to overcome, and people are making a fuss over her. It makes me feel so unimportant. And a little insecure."

"That explains it," Zach said thoughtfully.

"I think I also feel a little sorry for myself." Caroline shook her head. "I know it's dumb. But I can't help thinking it could have been me getting all the attention. Not from the tragedy—but because I really wanted to be different this year. More active. More outgoing. Now senior year is going to slip by without my ever becoming a real part of it. It's my last chance."

"If it helps, I know how you feel," Zach said kindly. "I always used to feel out of it in school."

"And now?"

Zach looked at her, surprised. "Now I'm not in school anymore, so it doesn't matter."

"You're not?"

"I thought you knew that. I graduated last year."

"You never said that. I thought you were a senior, like me."

"I don't have a category," he joked. "I'm taking this year to decide what I want to do next. I didn't want to go to college without knowing what I was there for."

"I can understand that," Caroline said. "College is a big commitment. You should get the most out of it."

"That's what I thought. I worked full-time this summer. Nothing great—mostly clerk-type stuff for a small publishing company. And since I'm only working there part time now, I thought I'd finally give acting a try—see if I should take it seriously."

"You should. You should give yourself a chance."

"You should too," Zach said. "You're too hard on yourself."

Caroline blushed. "My problems must seem pretty small compared to yours. You're trying to decide what to do with rest of your life."

"They don't seem small at all. I would probably feel the same way."

"I feel better just talking about it," Caroline admitted. She smiled. "So, Dr. Zach, what's the cure?"

Zach made a face. "Unfortunately, I don't know."

"You don't?"

"Sorry. I guess you'll have to figure that out yourself."

Crestfallen, Caroline slumped in her chair. "Oh, well. Maybe acting will help. I mean, I've always been so shy. It's funny, but in some ways, Chrissy fits in better than me. Even though she's from a farm, she can still act naturally with people from the city. I have a harder time feeling natural with everybody."

"Hey, no feeling sorry for yourself," Zach said.

"You're right. Rest time's over," she announced. "We haven't finished, you know. We've got to do our scene again—or did you forget?"

"I didn't forget," Zach said slowly. "I was trying to think of a way to help you."

Caroline pulled him off his chair. "Thanks, but like you said, I'll have to work it out myself." Nevertheless, she was glad to have someone on her side. Zach was turning into a real friend.

Chapter 8

As Caroline and Zach were finishing up their rehearsal, Mr. Kirby poked his head into the dining room.

"A lot of emoting coming out of here," he quipped. "Must be actors at work."

"Hi, Dad." Caroline put her script down. "We were just finishing this scene."

"Don't let me disturb you." Mr. Kirby held his hand out. "You must be Zach. Caroline has said nice things about you."

Bashfully, Zach shook hands. "Thanks. Uh, I'm glad to meet you."

"You kids go ahead." Mr. Kirby turned to leave the room.

"Wait, Dad. Let's see what my father thinks of the scene," she said to Zach.

Zach looked doubtful. "I don't think so, Cara. We haven't rehearsed enough."

Caroline laughed. "That's okay. My dad won't mind."

"Go on. I'd like to see it." Mr. Kirby pulled out a dining room chair.

"Yeah, come on, Zach," Caroline urged. "We'll do it with me being the girl and you the boy."

"Caroline . . ." Zach pulled her aside. "Your father is a professional critic."

"A music critic," Caroline pointed out, "not a drama critic."

"Cara, I don't mean to be a party pooper, but I'd really rather not do the scene for him just yet." Zach looked down at his feet. "I'm still not ready for an audience. Let's rehearse a bit more first, okay?"

Caroline shrugged and turned to her father. "We'll have to give you a rain check, Dad."

Laughing, Mr. Kirby got up. "I understand. Zach—I'd like to come when you and Caroline are in a finished play. If that's all right?"

"Sure," Zach said hastily. "That'd be great. A front row seat—and that's a promise. I just hate to perform without properly rehearsing first."

The front door slammed and Mr. Kirby peeked into the hall. "Chrissy's home," he announced.

"Oh?" Caroline busied herself straightening the dining room chairs. Her father called a hello down the hall and seconds later Chrissy appeared in the doorway.

"You're home late," Mr. Kirby said pleasantly. "Busy day?"

There was the usual bright smile on Chrissy's

face, but Caroline thought it looked a bit strained. It was hard to tell because Chrissy barely glanced at her. Caroline stiffened. It was so awful lately, with nothing quite normal between her and Chrissy. Luckily, she didn't think her parents had picked up on it.

"I got held up," Chrissy explained in her best, perky manner. "A make-up committee meeting."

Mr. Kirby nodded with interest. "That Senior Activities Committee we've heard so much about?"

Chrissy nodded enthusiastically.

"I hope it went well," Mr. Kirby said.

"Oh sure. I have plenty of volunteers," Chrissy said. "Everyone's making lists of things to do. It's going to be a great senior year."

"Isn't that nice," Caroline said stiffly. "Oh, by the way," she added politely, "this is my friend Zachary Landau. From the acting studio. Zach, this is my cousin Chrissy."

"Hello," Zach said, as polite and stiff as Caroline.

Chrissy gave him a wide grin. "Hi. It's great to meet you. Caroline hasn't said much about the acting workshop."

"She hasn't?" Zach replied casually.

Caroline was glad that Zach wasn't saying much either. She didn't want Chrissy poking her nose into *her* acting business. That was her own territory. It seemed funny not to confide in Chrissy, *but it's her own fault,* Caroline thought. She wasn't about to let Chrissy walk all over her without paying for it.

"Oh, I almost forgot. I have the mail." Chrissy dug through her pockets for several envelopes. "This is for you, Uncle Richard."

"Revisions." Mr. Kirby frowned. "I've been waiting for these. Back to work, I guess." Excusing himself, he went down the hall, muttering about fussy editors.

Alone with Chrissy and Zach, Caroline felt suddenly awkward. They both seemed to be waiting for her to say something.

"Any mail for me?" she asked, just to break the silence.

"Oh, yeah." Chrissy flipped through a handful of bills and envelopes. "A letter from Luke." Handing it over, she gave Caroline what was almost a smile.

Caroline glanced at Luke's familiar handwriting on the envelope, then put it carefully on the table to read later.

"Golly, Cara, aren't you going to read it now?"

"No, Chrissy, I'm not."

"That's pretty strange," Chrissy said pointedly.

"Not really," Caroline replied. She knew that Chrissy was wondering just what her relationship with Zach was, and the thought annoyed her. *Chrissy should mind her own business,* she thought angrily. "I'm busy right now. I'm rehearsing, in case you didn't know." She turned to Zach, speaking especially clearly. "It's a letter from my boyfriend in Iowa," she told him. That should satisfy her nosy cousin. After all, Caroline had nothing to hide.

"Iowa? Where Chrissy's from?" Zach asked. "Don't tell me your boyfriend is a farmer?" Zach laughed in surprise.

Both Caroline and Chrissy reacted. "What's wrong with Iowa?" Chrissy demanded.

"It's not funny," Caroline said at the same time. The two cousins looked at each other. For an instant, it was like old times—the two of them thinking the exact same thought at the same time. But the moment passed.

Zach flushed. "Nothing's wrong with Iowa. It just sounded funny," he explained. "Uh, it was the way she said it. Don't you think?" he asked hopefully.

Chrissy glared at him and Caroline rolled her eyes—the last thing she needed was a new feud with Chrissy.

"I'll leave you two *sophisticates* alone," Chrissy declared, stomping away.

"Chrissy, he didn't mean anything," Caroline began.

But Chrissy had already left the room. Caroline turned on Zach.

"Why'd you do that? You knew I was having trouble with Chrissy. Now she'll be impossible."

"It just slipped out," Zach said earnestly. "I'm sorry. I pictured you with this guy in a straw hat with hay sticking out of his teeth."

"Luke is nothing like that," Caroline protested.

"I'm really sorry. I hope it's no big deal."

"There's nothing wrong with being a farmer, you know."

"That's true," Zach admitted. "I was wrong, okay? I've never even been to a farm. What do I know? I didn't stop to think. I get tongue-tied in front of strangers, and I usually end up saying the wrong thing."

"Well, think *before* you speak next time, not afterward." Caroline folded her arms across her chest.

"Don't be mad," Zach pleaded. "I didn't mean anything."

Absent-mindedly, Caroline picked up the letter

again. Suddenly, she *did* want to read it.

"Zach, why don't we stop rehearsing for today?" she suggested. "We probably won't even be called on to do our scene this week."

Zach looked like she'd slapped him. "I'm sorry I insulted you before, Cara. I honestly didn't mean to make fun of your boyfriend. If—if you want to find a new acting partner, well, I understand."

"I do not want a new partner," Caroline said impatiently. "Let's just forget today, okay?"

"Okay," Zach said as he gathered his things together. "Well, I'd better go." He backed toward the door.

"Sure. I'll call you," Caroline said.

"Sure. See you."

Zach let himself out. Caroline knew she should have seen him to the door, or maybe apologized again, but she was just so darned annoyed.

She looked at the envelope she was clutching and suddenly she realized she hadn't been thinking of Luke at all lately. How was it possible? When she'd said goodbye to him after their incredible vacation in Hawaii, she'd thought they had a real future together. They'd decided that they would write once a week, and call when they could, and even apply to the same colleges together. At first, every minute away from Luke had driven her crazy. All she'd wanted was to be with him. And everything reminded her of him. But since school had started, he had gone completely out of her mind.

But a lot has happened lately and I've got so much on my mind. That's why I haven't thought about him. I still feel the same about Luke. I know I do.

Holding the letter, Caroline walked slowly to her bedroom. Chrissy had the stereo turned up so loud that Caroline winced. Really, it was too much sometimes. How could a person think with that noise blasting? Without a word to her cousin, she turned and went to the bathroom to read the letter. She sat cross-legged on the wide counter next to the sink, and slit open the envelope with her fingernail.

Dear Cara,
   Hi! How are you? I hope everything is good with you. I haven't gotten a letter in a while. How's your senior year going? So far, senior year at Danbury High is just like all the other years. Of course, everyone in town is still trying to straighten things out after the big twister. (ha ha!) My dad and I started building a new roof on the barn this week, so we're in pretty good shape.
   Well, that's about it for now. Take care.
                         Love,
                         Luke

Caroline folded the letter carefully and slipped it back in the envelope. Then she leaned back against the smooth tiles and stared at the flowers on the wallpaper opposite. It was nothing like Luke's old letters. Those had been filled with declarations—how much he missed her, how he couldn't wait to see her again. And he always signed his letters to her "All my love." Just plain "Love" was so impersonal—lots of people wrote "Love" on letters, even if they didn't mean it.

She sighed. It wasn't his fault. She was the one who hadn't written lately. It was so different in Hawaii. All she could think about was their plans for their future together. Now the future meant thinking about acting class and how she'd get through the year with Chrissy constantly stealing her thunder.

Caroline shifted. The bathroom was not the most comfortable place to think. She couldn't stay in there forever. And after all, she had a right to be in her own room!

Angrily, she stormed into the bedroom to find Chrissy sitting at *her* desk. Chrissy looked up, quickly folding away a letter.

Caroline glared at her. "Do you mind if I sit at my own desk?"

Chrissy sprang up. "Golly, take my head off, why don't you. There's a pile of junk on mine."

Well of course, Caroline thought wryly, pulling out the desk chair. *So what else is new?* Chrissy brushed past and sat on her bed, tucking the letter into the pocket of her jeans skirt.

Caroline hadn't meant to even speak to Chrissy, but curiosity got the better of her. "You got a letter too?"

"Uh huh," Chrissy nodded.

Caroline hesitated. She ought to ask if things were okay. "From your mom?"

"From Ben," Chrissy answered.

"Oh. Mine is from Luke."

"I know," Chrissy said.

Caroline bit her tongue. She was only trying to make polite conversation. "How is he?"

"Oh, he's fine," Chrissy said. She pursed her lips

as if she didn't want to talk either, but a moment later a torrent of words came spilling out as if she couldn't stop them.

"It's funny how a little thing like a tornado doesn't get Ben down. He's just upset about me staying here another whole year. He really wanted us to go to college together. *If* he even goes to college. He's thinking of taking a year off to work first," Chrissy paused, but only to take a breath. "Gosh, I still don't know what I want to do. I've become such a San Franciscan, now, you know? I hear great stuff about Berkeley and UCLA. Of course, UCLA is pretty far from here. I might want to stay closer to home. There are so many colleges in the Bay Area."

Caroline felt a sense of panic rising inside her. Then she felt ashamed of herself. This *was* Chrissy's home now—and who knew for how long? But college in the Bay Area! Caroline felt terrified. What if Chrissy never left! What if she was always there, a shadow over Caroline's entire life.

"But, what about Ben? You two are so close. You really want to be together, don't you?" Cara asked hopefully.

"Oh, I don't know," Chrissy answered with a shrug. "Maybe it's not such a good idea."

"You used to think it was," Caroline pointed out. Secretly, she was shocked. If Chrissy was undecided about Ben—her steady boyfriend (minus a few months) since eighth grade—how could Caroline ever decide about Luke?

"I'm really involved in things here," Chrissy was saying. "I have a lot of friends here now. After two years, no one in Danbury will even remember me. I'm really out of it there."

Caroline's mind was racing. On the one hand, she felt sorry for Chrissy. There was a lot of truth in what she was saying. After two years away, she wouldn't be part of her old home town. Still, having Chrissy around her neck for the rest of her life wasn't a very happy prospect either.

Chrissy looked up curiously. "So where do you think you'll apply to school? We don't have much time left to decide."

"I still don't know," Caroline said hastily. She gave a nervous laugh. "*Mon dieu*—so many decisions to make!" She could see her whole senior year ruined, and then her college career—all dominated by Chrissy. Chrissy getting into every course she wanted to get into. Chrissy getting the dorm room Caroline had her heart set on. Chrissy on every freshman committee Caroline was interested in! She knew it was ridiculous, but she couldn't help feeling that way.

"Truthfully, Chrissy—I haven't made up my mind. I don't even have an idea of what to major in."

"I see," Chrissy said thoughtfully. "I guess it would be hard for you to decide. Especially if you get really serious about your acting."

"I guess that's possible," Caroline said.

Chrissy looked at her coyly. "Your friend Zach seems pretty interested in you."

Caroline frowned as she straightened up a few papers on the corner of her desk. "He's not. Not that way. In fact, we just met last week. We're only friends."

"And that's all?"

"What are you, a watchdog or something?" Caroline felt a burst of annoyance.

"I just wondered. You keep saying you're still going with Luke, but you hardly mention him anymore."

"You never mention Ben, either."

"I don't?" Chrissy was suddenly silent.

"We both have a lot on our minds," Caroline finally said.

Chrissy shrugged. "I guess so. I guess it's hard finding time to keep up a long-distance romance when you're active on senior class committees."

"I wouldn't know," Caroline said. She didn't bother to hide the hurt in her voice, but Chrissy didn't even seem to notice.

"Well, you probably want to be alone and here I am, taking up all your time, as usual." Chrissy bounced off the bed. "I'll be in the kitchen, if anyone wants me."

Caroline stared after her. Chrissy was right—she did want to be alone, and she was grateful for the quiet. Sometimes she didn't understand her cousin at all. Just when she was the most annoyed with her, Chrissy did something sweet or thoughtful. *She's going to drive me up a wall one of these days*, Caroline predicted, shaking her head in puzzlement.

Chapter 9

The blissful silence of the bedroom didn't last long. Little more than half an hour later, Chrissy burst in. "Cara—you won't believe it!"

Caroline suppressed a groan. *So much for privacy.*

"Your mom just got home from the gallery," Chrissy said breathlessly.

Caroline stared at her cousin as if she'd lost her mind. "She comes home every night."

Chrissy's flushed cheeks got even brighter. "I don't mean *that's* the news." Dropping onto the bed, she took a deep breath. "It's fantastic," she bubbled. "We've all been invited to a super posh opening at an art gallery."

"Chrissy, I've been to at least one gala opening a year for as long as I can remember."

"Yes, but this is an invitation to dinner afterwards—at Felicia Halloran's house. You know, the woman who owns the Halloran gallery?"

"Of course I know who she is," Caroline said. "I took you there your first week in town, remember? She only runs the hottest gallery in the city."

"Right! Isn't it fantastic! Your mom said it's an honor to be asked there."

"I guess so," Caroline said. It was hard to be excited about the invitation. After all, her mother knew all the gallery owners in San Francisco. "I stopped getting excited about those things years ago. And I don't feel like going to another dull party."

"Well, I guess I'm not as worldly as you." Chrissy picked at a loose thread on the bedspread.

Caroline felt a stab of remorse. She didn't really have to rain on Chrissy's parade. "You know, Ms. Halloran's house is incredible. It's in Pacific Heights. Ultra-modern. A really famous architect designed it."

"Really?" Chrissy perked up.

"Actually, I've always wanted to see it from the inside," Caroline added. "Is it going to be a fancy dinner party, or just a few people?"

"I'm not sure," Chrissy said. "But it is a fantastic invitation, isn't it?"

"Sure." Caroline smiled suddenly. "Remember the reception we had here once, and you thought the sculpture was a pile of garbage?" She giggled, remembering the artist's stunned reaction.

Chrissy giggled too. "That was a hoot. Everyone thought it was funny. And his sculpture *did* look like a pile of trash."

"I just hope you don't do anything like that this time. I'd die of embarrassment."

"Golly, Cara—I'm completely cool about those things now." Chrissy grinned. "So you are going to go to the dinner, aren't you?"

"Oh, why not. It'll be worth it to see the inside of that house."

"Great!" Chrissy sat up on the bed and grinned. Her eyes shone with excitement. "It'll be loads more fun if you come with us. You know how your mom and dad are—they always meet lots of people they know and start gabbing away."

Caroline bristled. It wasn't as if Chrissy was taking her parents away from her, but it sure sounded like it.

"Of course I'll go," Caroline declared firmly. "It's certainly an honor for mom to be invited to Ms. Halloran's with her whole family."

"To tell you the truth, Aunt Edith is thrilled, but I think it's more than the honor." Chrissy lowered her voice. "I think your mom wants to work for Ms. Halloran. She said that Ms. Halloran is looking for someone to organize new exhibitions at her gallery. I think that's why she's so excited about this. That's why she wants us to make a good impression, too."

"Oh, I doubt that." Caroline laughed awkwardly. "Mom likes the gallery she's at now. Even if she got a big raise for switching jobs, I don't think she'd go for it."

"You didn't hear the way she sounded when she told me about this, Cara. She was saying that it would be a terrific opportunity. I really think I'm right."

"Chrissy, I'm sure I would know. Mom would have mentioned something to me." Caroline tapped her pen impatiently on the desk.

"We'll see," Chrissy said mysteriously.

Caroline hid the annoyance she felt. "Anyway, when is this extravaganza?"

"Wednesday night. A school night!"

"We've stayed out late on school nights before," Caroline reminded her.

"I know," Chrissy said airily, "but this school night is different."

Caroline tapped the pen faster. "Why is this Wednesday different?"

"Well, I don't always have a breakfast meeting the next day," Chrissy answered.

"Breakfast meeting?"

Chrissy beamed with pride. "You kind of gave me the idea. With the coffee hour—what a disaster that was, remember? But then I thought, why waste the hours before school starts? Everyone's always hanging around that little coffee shop, grabbing something to eat. So I thought, why not have weekly coffee hours in the morning, instead of after school when kids have other things to do?"

Caroline frowned and abruptly stopped tapping her pen. Her idea had been a good one. If she had been running the meeting, instead of Chrissy, things would have gone right the first time.

"It may be the best idea I ever had," Chrissy said. She leaped up and started pulling clothes from her closet.

"Now what are you doing?"

"I must be losing my mind! I promised Aunt Edith

I'd look through my clothes. I don't have a thing to wear to Halloran's."

"You have plenty of things. Wear your yellow dress. Or what about your new blue one?"

"That thing? I've only worn it about a million times. Besides, that old stain never came out."

"What stain?"

Chrissy shook her head at Caroline. "You were right there! I wore it for Tracy's birthday, at that fancy Chinese restaurant. Duck sauce, all over." Chrissy held the dress up. A huge dark blotch ruined the skirt.

"Chrissy! Didn't you soak it when we got home?"

"I guess I forgot."

It was so typical of Chrissy to forget. "Wear the yellow, then. It looks fine."

"What are you going to wear?" Chrissy gnawed her fingernails.

"I don't know. Something." Caroline shrugged. She wasn't in the mood to talk about what to wear on Wednesday.

"Like, maybe your white suit?"

"Maybe."

Chrissy groaned. "Oh no."

"What's wrong now?"

"Cara—that suit is silk."

"So?"

"So, I don't have anything nearly as nice as real silk! It's so fancy and it's . . . it's so sophisticated. I suppose you're going to wear your pearls with it?"

"I usually do." Caroline had always been proud of herself in that outfit—it made her feel elegant and grown up.

Chrissy looked crestfallen. "You'll look beautiful."

"So will you," Caroline assured her. "Besides, these openings are always so crowded, no one will even be able to see you."

"How about the dinner party? People will see me then, and I'll look like a geek next to you."

"You will not."

Chrissy grabbed an armful of dresses. "I'm going to see what Aunt Edith thinks."

"Oh, Chrissy—she'll think the same as me. Your yellow is perfect. You look great in it."

"I'll see."

Caroline let out a huge sigh as Chrissy whirled out the door. She had too much on her mind to think about dresses. What she really had to do was think about Luke's letter. How in the world should she answer him?

'Dear Luke, How are you, I am fine' was too stuffy and formal. 'Dear Luke, I was so glad to get your letter' gave a false impression, like she'd been sitting around waiting for it. Actually, she was the one who owed him a letter.

Frowning, she tapped her pen against her chin. *I'm sure it's supposed to be easier than this to write a letter to your boyfriend.*

Finally she took a sheet of her good stationery out of the drawer. Pale blue, with her name and address embossed in darker blue at the top, it had taken her months to save the money for it. If she used her good stationery, she'd have to try extra hard not to make mistakes.

I'll be completely truthful, she decided. *That's always best when you don't know how to handle a situation.*

Pleased with this sensible solution, she bent her

head over the page and wrote with determination.

> Dear Luke,
> I know I owe you a letter. To be perfectly honest, I've been so caught up in things that I simply forgot to write. I'm sorry. I know that isn't fair to you, especially now with the excitement and trouble from the tornado to deal with. I don't have a better excuse.

She stared at her neat penmanship. She couldn't possibly send him this! He'd think she was completely self-centered and she didn't want that—although she supposed she had been a bit self-centered lately. Besides, it made it sound like she'd forgotten him, and she definitely didn't want him to think that. She felt the same about him as ever.

With a sigh, she crumpled the good piece of paper and tossed it in the trashbasket. She pulled out a fresh sheet and started over again.

> Dear Luke,
> Thanks for your letter. I know it was my turn to write, but things have been crazy here. Of course, you know that Chrissy is now staying for another year. It's been very hard for me to get used to the idea. Chrissy and I normally get along really well, but lately, well, she's really getting on my nerves. I think it has to do with this committee I wanted to run. . .

This was even worse that the last! Disgusted, Caroline tore the sheet of paper into tiny pieces. All she needed was for Chrissy or her mother or someone to find it and read it! Feeling completely frustrated, she threw her pen down and slammed her desk drawer closed.

This is ridiculous! I know Luke—I can be honest with him. Why is this so hard?

Just as she was reaching for another sheet of stationery, Chrissy came bouncing back into the room. Caroline tried not to look annoyed. Chrissy was even more excited than she was before, if that was possible.

"Cara, you won't believe it, I am just the luckiest girl on the face of the earth!" Talking a blue streak before she got through the door, Chrissy unceremoniously dropped her clothes into a heap on the floor. "I was right! Aunt Edith doesn't think the yellow is good enough. I don't have anything that will do at all. So, guess what?"

Caroline didn't bother answering. She knew Chrissy would answer the question before she had a chance to open her mouth, and that's exactly what Chrissy did.

"She decided I need something new! We're going shopping, just the two of us. Just for this occasion, can you believe it? Though of course, I'm sure I'll wear whatever I get again. I mean, after all, it'll probably be something as beautiful as your white silk suit, and you don't just wear something like that once. That's a classic, isn't it? Holy mazoley, Cara, your mom is absolutely the best aunt in the whole universe!"

Caroline felt breathless just listening to her cousin.

"We're going to have lunch at Top of the Mark

and everything. I've never been there! Oh, Cara—is it as special as they say?"

Caroline raised her eyebrows. "It's mostly for tourists, actually. I'd much rather go to the Garden Court for lunch. It's so classy."

"Yes, but the Mark Hopkins is the best hotel in San Francisco, and there's supposed to be a terrific view from the restaurant. Aunt Edith is so good to me!"

"She is, isn't she," Caroline agreed. "Excuse me a minute, Chrissy. I just remembered something I forgot to tell Mom."

Her mother was relaxing in the living room, idly stirring a cup of coffee. Caroline sat near her.

"Hi, honey. I'm bushed! I could use a vacation."

"You work hard setting up those exhibits at the gallery, don't you, Mom?"

Her mother smiled. "Yes, I think so, but it's worth the work." She paused and set her cup down. "What's on your mind, honeybun?"

Caroline blushed. "Mom, don't think I'm being selfish or anything, but if Chrissy's getting a new outfit for this opening, shouldn't I have one too? The truth is, I've been to tons more openings than Chrissy and I nearly always wear the same thing. People will remember my suit."

"That suit is beautiful on you," her mother said. "And it never goes out of style."

"That's the trouble. I'd rather wear something more stylish, but none of my other clothes are as good as that."

Her mother leaned her head against the back of the sofa, briefly closing her eyes. "Cara, if you have the money to buy a new outfit, then go ahead. You don't need my permission."

"You know I don't have enough money for a really good outfit, Mom." Caroline took a deep breath. "Chrissy doesn't have enough money either, but she's getting a new outfit anyway."

"That's because she has nothing to wear for Wednesday. And maybe it will boost her spirits to get dressed up in something new," Caroline's mother replied wearily.

"Well then, how about boosting my spirits with a new pair of shoes or a blouse?" Caroline ventured.

"Caroline Kirby, what has gotten into you?" her mother snapped. "Don't you have any sympathy for your cousin at all?"

Caroline stood up and put her hands on her hips. "I can't believe this. Chrissy complains and gets a whole new outfit. I'm your own daughter, and I make a simple request for new shoes, and you act like I'm a spoiled brat."

"I don't like you to pout, Cara." Her mother sat up straighter. "You have so many nice things. Do you really think you need something new? Honestly?"

"I don't *need* it," Caroline admitted. "But it would be nice."

"Maybe another time," her mother said.

Caroline thought about it. "Maybe I should come along," she finally said. "In case Chrissy gets strange notions about what to get. You might need me to help talk her out of something."

Her mother hesitated. "Actually, sweetheart, I wanted to treat Chrissy to a special trip. I think she could use it."

"All I ever hear is poor Chrissy," Caroline exploded. "You'd think people would be tired of feeling sorry for her already!"

"I think you're feeling sorry for yourself, Cara, and I'm losing my patience with you," her mother warned.

With great effort, Caroline controlled herself. "I'm sorry. I didn't mean to sound so awful. But it seems like everyone's going out of their way to be nice to her, and I get left behind!"

"I don't believe that."

"It's true," Caroline cried.

"Give me an example."

"Well . . ." Caroline wanted to tell her mother about the Senior Activities Committee and what a fiasco it had turned out to be, how Chrissy had stolen her big dream—but her mother would probably think she was being selfish or childish or just plain jealous.

"Well, for example, the day we went to Mount Tamalpais." Now that she had started, Caroline felt foolish. "We were supposed to bring the desserts, and Chrissy forgot and left them here. Then, when we got to the mountain, everyone thought I forgot them and yelled at me. But when it turned out to be Chrissy," she ended lamely, "they, uh, they just apologized and said they didn't need dessert anyway."

"They were being kind," her mother told her. "It's to their credit. Your friends are good people."

"I know, but . . ." Caroline trailed off. It sounded ridiculous to her too, now. How could she explain how hurt and angry she had been at the time?

Her mother's voice was softer now. "Cara, you know Chrissy's parents are very proud people. Too proud to take our money to help them. Taking care of Chrissy is the least we can do. If your Aunt Ingrid knows Chrissy is happy, that will make her feel better."

"I know," Caroline muttered.

"Ingrid wasn't very happy to have Chrissy stay here another year. She was really looking forward to having her home again," Caroline's mother said. "I'd hate it if you couldn't come home after a whole year away."

"I'd hate it too," Cara admitted. "I see your point. I'm sorry for what I said." She leaned over to give her mother a quick hug, then headed down the hall to the bedroom with a lighter heart.

She found Chrissy sprawled on the bed, surrounded by sheets of paper.

"What are you doing?" Caroline asked.

"Writing my folks about the big party and the special shopping trip. They really get a kick out of city things like that. I know it sounds ordinary to you, but art openings and buffets at Top of the Mark are pretty far out for people in Danbury."

"Chrissy, I'm sorry if I acted badly before. It *is* exciting to go to this party. Even for me."

Chrissy looked surprised. "That's okay. You don't have to apologize or anything." Smiling, she turned back to her letter writing.

Caroline pulled her bank book from its hiding place. She had just enough money left to get Chrissy that fabulous pair of earrings they saw in Union Square. Actually, she had better wait to see what kind of outfit Chrissy bought, and then she would treat her to some nice jewelry to go with it. Just the thought of doing something generous made her feel better. And it had been a long time since she'd felt that good about herself.

Maybe now is a good time to write my letter to Luke, she decided.

Chrissy was an absolute inspiration for writing, the way her pen zipped over the page. Caroline felt silly for ever having trouble writing Luke. Resolutely, she pulled open her desk drawer and took out her good stationery again.

Dear Luke,
Thanks for your letter. It was nice of you not to mention that it was my turn to write. I let myself get caught up in other things and I'm afraid I neglected you. I'm sorry, and it won't happen again.
Let me tell you what I've been so 'caught up' in!

As she wrote a long description of her acting class, she couldn't help feeling that maybe things had taken a turn for the better.

Chapter 10

On Saturday morning the fog had rolled in thick around the house. Chrissy had left early on her shopping expedition with Caroline's mother, and Caroline drifted restlessly around her room. It was ridiculous; she had so much studying to do, but somehow, she couldn't get started. Her mind felt as foggy as the streets outside. Maybe when the fog cleared up, her mind would clear up as well.

In the meantime, she decided, it was silly to waste the day. If she couldn't get started on school work, she might as well clean up her room.

Not my idea of a perfect Saturday, but at least I'll be doing something constructive, she told herself.

Halfheartedly, she began pulling things out of her closet. Just as she had them sorted into 'mend, iron, or wash' piles, the doorbell rang.

"Tracy! What are you doing here?"

"Surprise!" Tracy grinned at her. "Feel like a visit?"

"Do I ever! I am so glad to see someone."

Tracy struggled out of her rain poncho. "Where is everyone around here?"

"Mom and Chrissy are out. My dad's on deadline and I have strict instructions not to bother him." She peered at her friend closely. "You look winded. What's up?"

Tracy gestured at the street. "Rode my bike over. I really needed exercise, you know? I think I did about five miles."

"In this fog? You're crazy."

"I know," Tracy grinned, "but I practically had the streets to myself. I think most of the city decided not to get out of bed today." She glanced behind her. "I locked my bike to that street light. Think it'll be okay? I couldn't face your front steps."

"I don't blame you." Caroline grinned. The steep stairs up to the front porch of the Kirbys' apartment house were enough to discourage anyone, much less someone who'd just ridden five miles of San Francisco's hills.

Tracy pushed up the sleeves of her sweatshirt. "Do you have any cold juice in the house? I'm steaming."

"Sure. Come on in. I'll get you a drink."

Tracy followed her up to the third floor apartment and into the spacious kitchen. She perched on the edge of a chair while Caroline fetched glasses. "Where'd Chrissy go? She's not out running in this fog too, is she?"

"Not today. One crazy person is enough." Caroline grabbed the juice and a couple of muffins from the refrigerator. "She's with my mom. Big shopping trip."

Tracy wrinkled her nose quizzically. "With your mom? How come you didn't go too?"

"It's sort of a special treat," Caroline explained. "We're all invited to a big art opening and dinner party. I already have something to wear, but Mom thought Chrissy should have something new."

"Wow. Lucky Chrissy."

"Yeah." Caroline stared at the glass in her hands. "It's too bad I couldn't talk her into something new for me." She sighed. "But my house wasn't blown away in a tornado."

Tracy gave her a curious look.

"The thing is," Caroline explained slowly, "Chrissy didn't so much *need* a new dress. Mom just wanted to treat her to something special. So they're going shopping and out to lunch at Top of the Mark."

"I thought people only went there after proms and things like that," Tracy teased.

"Like I said, it's a special treat."

"Is Chrissy still upset about the tornado?" Tracy asked. "I thought she was taking it pretty well now."

"She is," Caroline assured her, "but Mom still wanted to do something extra-nice for her. So she feels this is the least she can do."

Tracy nodded. "That sounds like your mom."

Caroline watched Tracy thoughtfully. "Then you don't think she's going overboard?"

"What do you mean?"

"Pampering Chrissy," Caroline said carefully. "I mean, it's been weeks since the tornado. Chrissy must be over it by now."

"It's not so much the tornado," Tracy answered. "It's having to stay here. She wanted to go back to Danbury so badly."

"She's hardly suffering." Caroline pulled her chair closer to the table, leaning on her elbows. "Everyone here was thrilled she's staying. It's not like she's being punished, or anything. I mean, this isn't exactly a prison."

Tracy shrugged. "I know. And I'm sure Chrissy feels at home here, but . . ."

"But what?" Caroline peered anxiously into her friend's eyes.

"But it's still not her house. It's yours, and Chrissy is the visitor."

"I see." Caroline sat back. So Tracy still believed that Chrissy deserved special attention.

Maybe I'm being blind, or selfish. Am I the only one who thinks all this fuss is silly?

"Anyway," Tracy said brightly, "I didn't come all this way in the fog to talk about Chrissy."

"Is something special on your mind?" Caroline asked.

"Some*one* special." Tracy grinned. "Tony Boyd."

Tony Boyd was a real hunk—also smart, and funny. Everyone at Maxwell liked him, and Caroline knew of lots of girls who had crushes on him. But he was in a different crowd than Caroline's, so she had never gotten to know him very well.

"What about him?"

"What if I said I thought he liked me?" Dimples appeared in Tracy's cheeks, setting off her sparkling brown eyes. Caroline suddenly thought how very pretty her friend was.

"Well, does he?" she asked. "Or are you just wishing he did?"

"I'll know Monday. I'm supposed to meet him in the library. Either he wants to pick my brain about our science paper, or he really likes me." Tracy nearly clapped her hands in excitement.

Caroline stared. "You and Tony? When did all this happen? How?"

Tracy winked. "Pretty unbelievable, huh? Ask Chrissy, she knows all about it."

"Chrissy does?"

"In a way, she sort of made it happen. I mean, I always liked Tony, but I was too shy to do anything about it. Then Chrissy found out, and the next thing I knew, she had him convinced I was the only one in school who could help him on this project of his."

"But you didn't tell me you liked Tony Boyd," Caroline said.

Tracy's eyes were positively dancing. "Well, now you know."

"And Chrissy got you together?"

Tracy cautioned her. "We're hardly together. But still, it's fantastic, isn't it? I can't wait 'til Monday."

"I don't blame you," Caroline said lamely. "I'll keep my fingers crossed for you."

Why didn't Tracy tell me she liked Tony? Caroline wondered. *We've been best friends forever—she should have told me, not Chrissy.* She felt almost sick to her stomach. *Why am I left out of everything important?*

"That's terrific," she managed to tell Tracy. "I really hope it works out for you." She squeezed Tracy's arm.

"Thanks. Tony's great, isn't he? I think he's one of the smartest kids in school."

"*You're* one of the smartest kids in school," Caroline pointed out.

"Well . . ." Tracy blushed. "Don't you think we'll make a perfect couple? Chrissy and I have it all figured out—I'll just keep asking him for study dates. Things are bound to get serious if he's around me enough." She gave Caroline a teasing look. "You know how irresistible I am."

Caroline laughed in agreement. "Your parents will flip out. They think you're too young to be interested in *any* boy, no matter how smart he is."

Tracy rolled her eyes. "Tell me about it. They seriously think I'm going to spend my last year in high school buried behind a stack of textbooks! I mean, I do want good grades and I do want to go to a top college, and I know my future's at stake and all that, but that has nothing to do with Tony. No way am I going to miss a chance to have the best year I ever had at Maxwell. No way."

Caroline agreed with Tracy. She also believed in academic excellence, and worked hard for her good grades. It was almost a matter of personal pride. And with a super guy like Tony to study with, it wouldn't seem like such a chore. She hoped Tracy's parents would see it that way.

"Tracy, wouldn't it be great to go to a real air-head school? I mean, with no academic pressure at all?"

"You'd hate it," Tracy scoffed.

"Maybe not. I'd be a completely different person." Caroline shut her eyes dreamily. "I'd have fun, fun, fun. I'd do nothing but chase boys and go to parties.

Maybe I'd be a cheerleader or something."

Tracy laughed. "You're not the type."

"Sure I am," Caroline protested. "What about my dancing and my acting—I love to perform. And I'm just as athletic as any cheerleader."

Tracy peered at her. "I think you're serious."

"I am," Caroline insisted. "Just once, I'd like to have fun. I'd really like to be someone else. I mean, here it is, senior year, and I'm missing out on all the good times at school. I want to really make my mark at Maxwell, be a real part of the senior class. That would be so great."

"You don't really mean it," Tracy said.

"I do."

Tracy got a worried look on her face. "Cara—are you still mad at me about the committee? Because I gave Chrissy the idea to take the job? Is that what you mean about being part of the senior class?"

"Oh, no," Caroline assured her. "It's not that. I'm over that now. Really, it has nothing to do with you."

Tracy looked relieved. "Thank goodness. I thought I'd ruined your whole senior year."

"You couldn't," Caroline answered. "Look, Trace, I admit it upset me a lot at first. I was hurt when Chrissy got the job instead of me, especially when you suggested it. But I'm over that now."

"I'm so glad. I'd never do anything to hurt you, Cara."

"I know."

Tracy leaned over and gave Caroline a big hug. Caroline hugged her back, but she couldn't help wondering if things were the same between them. Was Chrissy closer to Tracy now than she was?

Caroline was used to sharing her room with Chrissy by now—but she didn't think she could share her best friend!

"When do you think Chrissy will get home?" Tracy asked, as if reading Caroline's mind.

"Not until later," Caroline said. "Tracy, what do you think of this idea? I thought I'd buy Chrissy something to go with her new outfit. Earrings, or a necklace or something. Maybe you could help me pick it out."

"I'd love to!" Tracy replied. "That way I could thank Chrissy for helping me with Tony."

The girls were quiet then, as they finished off the muffins and emptied out the container of orange juice.

"I hope things work out with Tony," Tracy said, putting down her empty glass. She had a worried expression on her face.

"If he's as smart as you say, then you've got it made," Caroline reassured her friend. "He'd be pretty dumb not to see how terrific you are."

"Thanks Cara," Tracy said, then she paused. "Hey, I have an idea. Let's go shopping tonight. We could go to that really neat boutique on Haight Street."

"Perfect! We're sure to find something there that Chrissy would like," Caroline added.

"And then coffee and a pastry at one of those cafés," Tracy put in. "Oh—you didn't have other plans, did you?" Tracy frowned.

"None," Caroline said. "This is perfect. We haven't done anything special together in ages."

Tracy nodded. "I know. I guess we've both been caught up in different things. From now on, we'll

both make more of an effort to spend time together."

"You're right," Caroline said. "It's a deal."

Chapter 11

Caroline was changing to go meet Tracy that evening when Chrissy got home. She burst into the bedroom, bundles cradled in both arms.

"Cara! You won't believe the great stuff I got!"

She dumped packages onto the bed. "We bought so much," Chrissy exclaimed. "I've never had so much fun in my life."

Breathlessly, she held up a stunning silk outfit. It was pale yellow, only a few shades lighter than the yellow dress already hanging in Chrissy's closet, but perfect with her blonde hair and blue eyes.

"I had your white suit in mind," she admitted, "but we thought this was more my style."

It was a two piece outfit with a loose, free top floating over a long full skirt.

"It's much less tailored that yours, but Aunt Edith says it's just as elegant. It's a very fine fabric,"

Chrissy went on, rubbing a bit of material between her thumb and forefinger. "Feel that 'hand.'"

"I can tell you were shopping with Mom," Caroline teased. "You sound just like her."

She could imagine the shopping trip—her mother choosing dresses from the racks and inspecting the quality of the fabric and workmanship before handing the outfits to Chrissy to try on. Then she would tell Chrissy exactly how she thought the dress looked—even if Chrissy didn't want to hear it.

"Aunt Edith was terrific," Chrissy enthused. "We had this one really nasty saleslady in Magnin's, and your mom cut her right down to size. Gosh, she has wonderful taste! I had a ball, Cara. Your mom let me try on these outrageous outfits I would never actually buy—it was hysterical. Oh, and can you believe the ladies room in that store? I never saw so much marble in my life! And all those mirrors and fresh flowers! I thought I'd made a mistake and was in a private suite or something!" Chrissy giggled.

Caroline felt a pang of jealousy. She knew exactly what Chrissy was talking about. What fun it would have been to be there while Chrissy raved and giggled over everything.

"I mean, Caroline, I thought I'd seen just about everything there was to see in San Francisco—but now I know I've just barely scratched the surface!"

"I love your dress," Caroline said, trying to get Chrissy back on the subject. "What did you get to go with it?"

"Everything!" Chrissy began tearing into packages. "Oh, and our lunch," she suddenly gasped, forgetting all about her purchases. "It was fabulous! We had this incredible view. We saw the house and everything. And I adored the little glass elevator that takes you up there—I felt just like I was in a grain elevator going to the top of a silo! It almost made me homesick."

Caroline looked at her cousin in concern.

"Only kidding," Chrissy assured her. "It was a perfect day. And after we found my dress—which wasn't easy, believe me—we went for shoes and a bag. I'm bushed!"

Chrissy flung herself against the pillows.

"I guess shopping can be hard work sometimes," Caroline said.

"I'll be awfully glad to get back into jeans and hi-tops again," Chrissy agreed.

Caroline picked up a shoe box. "Can I see?"

"Help yourself," Chrissy said grandly, sprawling against the bed. "I'm too pooped to look at another thing."

Carefully, Caroline took out the pair of white kid pumps. They had slender straps and a delicate high heel. "These are gorgeous," she said, trying not to think of the old patent leather she always wore with her white suit.

"Look at the bag," Chrissy directed. "That's really gorgeous. I thought I'd have to get a matching clutch or some old lady thing, but your mom let me get this fabulous shoulder bag."

"It is fabulous," Caroline agreed, pulling out a small pouch on a long strap. The bag was sewn together out of patches of leather; white kid, shiny silver, and even pale yellow snakeskin.

"It matches perfectly," Chrissy exclaimed, "and it isn't in the least bit stuffy."

"It's terrific." Caroline laid the shoes and purse

alongside the new dress and studied the effect. It was at once elegant and funky—and totally unlike anything Caroline owned.

"I'll put them away for you," she offered. Carefully, she hung the delicate silk outfit, pushing things out of the way to make space among the clutter in Chrissy's end of the closet.

"I guess I'll clean that mess up soon," Chrissy promised. "I have to take good care of my new things."

Caroline stashed the shoes in their box and put the new bag on a shelf.

"Throw me my jeans and stuff, will you, Cara?"

With a weary sigh Chrissy yanked off her cotton skirt and blouse and pulled on her jeans and favorite oversized sweatshirt. "Whew—I feel like me again."

"You'll have to try it all on," Caroline told her. "I'm dying to see what it looks like."

"Later," Chrissy pleaded. "I've about had my fill of being a lady today."

"Okay. Anyway, I'm late." Caroline finished putting on her makeup and tucked in her shirt.

Chrissy sat up on the bed. "Are you going out?"

Caroline froze. "Oh, uh—no place special. Why? You don't want to go—do you?" She held her breath and stared at her cousin. She'd just assumed Chrissy would be so tired from her long day of shopping that she'd want to stay home. She couldn't come with Tracy and her! It would ruin the whole surprise!

"Uh, I'm just meeting Tracy," Caroline stammered, feeling her face grow warm. She was no good at fibbing. "We may go out for a while later tonight."

"Oh yeah? Like where?"

"I'm not sure," Caroline said vaguely. "Maybe to the Haight."

"The Haight! That's my favorite. I love going there."

"That's news to me. You always said it made you uncomfortable—all those old hippies and street people roaming around."

"That's when I was new here," Chrissy pointed out. "I don't mind anymore. Besides, it'd be a blast to go with you and Tracy."

"But you're exhausted," Caroline reminded her. "You didn't want to move."

"I'm all right. I just got my second wind," Chrissy declared.

"Chrissy," Caroline began, a little desperately, "don't you have stuff to do? I mean, you must have committee activities to go over. And you didn't get a thing done all day."

Chrissy opened her mouth to protest but then a look of understanding appeared on her face. "Oh, I get it. That's okay, I understand if you want Tracy to yourself."

"That's not it," Caroline objected. Although that wasn't the main reason why she didn't want her cousin around, it was true that Caroline didn't want to share Tracy tonight. The thought made her feel guilty—and mean.

It can be as good a surprise with Chrissy there, I suppose.

She paused as she zipped up her denim jacket. "Listen, Chrissy, you should come. I really did think you'd be tired. If you're not, please come along."

"Oh, no. I don't want to be a wet blanket. This is your night with Tracy."

"It's not like that at all," Caroline insisted. "Come on—only hurry, I was supposed to leave ten minutes ago."

"Well, okay then!" In a flash, Chrissy was off the bed and down the hall, grabbing a sweater on the way.

Caroline shook her head fondly. Sometimes, there was just no resisting Chrissy's enthusiasm.

The Haight was bustling with a Saturday night crowd. Locals and tourists thronged the streets, peeking into boutiques, browsing in the bookshops, and filling the cafes.

"You're sure you know where you're going," Chrissy asked again as Caroline led the girls up a narrow side street.

"Exactly," Caroline assured her. She stopped in front of a small store halfway up a steep block. "Tracy and I found this place by accident one day," she told Chrissy. "Isn't it super?"

The girls crowded into the shop. It was filled with unusual handmade items of every description. "Super," Chrissy agreed, "but what are we supposed to get here?" She picked up a hand-carved ivory backscratcher and pretended to scratch Tracy's head with it. "New ideas?"

Caroline laughed. "More like new earrings. I'll show you—out back." She led the way past cluttered shelves to a small cleared out space in the back of the store. There was one display case there crammed with eye-catching jewelry. Next to it was a small table and mirror where customers could sit and try things on.

"The woman who runs the place makes these herself," Caroline explained. "I love these necklaces, don't you?"

She held up a rope of crystal beads, fastened at the neck with a large enamel flower. "You wear it backwards, with the flower clasp in front," she explained, draping it over her head. She showed them how the necklace was long enough to wrap or even tie in knots.

"It's gorgeous," Tracy breathed. She threw Caroline a look of approval. They both knew that anything they bought would really be for Chrissy.

"I've had my eye on it for a while," Caroline said, "but I needed a special occasion." She turned to Chrissy. "Do you like it too?"

"It's nice," Chrissy said, barely glancing at the necklace, "but look at these wild earrings!" She held up a pair of gaudy rhinestone earrings. "They really shine."

Caroline frowned, whispering to Tracy. "They don't go with her new outfit at all. And my mother would hate them."

"They're wild all right," Tracy told Chrissy hastily, "but the necklace is much prettier. And better. You can do so many things with it."

"Like what?" Chrissy looked perplexed. "Don't you just wear it?"

Caroline rolled her eyes. "Of course."

"I mean, you can wear it so many different ways," Tracy continued.

"I don't care about that. If I were buying something, I'd get these earrings." Chrissy held them up, admiring her reflection in the mirror. "They'd be great with my new outfit."

Caroline shot Tracy a helpless look. "Uh, actually, maybe you'd better get Mom's opinion. I mean, after all that shopping today, she might be insulted if you bought something for the dinner without her."

"You think so?" Reluctantly, Chrissy put the earrings back.

"But Chrissy, I was thinking of getting something new to wear with my white suit," Caroline said. "Don't you think this necklace would go well with that?"

Chrissy nodded. "I see," she said tactfully. "You're right, Cara—the necklace is fine. And I don't need these earrings. I have enough new things."

Turning to Tracy, Chrissy lowered her voice, but Caroline could still hear her.

"Now I get it," Chrissy whispered. "And I don't blame Cara for being jealous. Aunt Edith did spend a fortune on me, and I guess it's only natural that Cara wants something new for herself."

Caroline flushed with embarrassment, but she could hardly tell Chrissy the truth. It would spoil the surprise.

"I don't think she's jealous," Tracy whispered back. Caroline felt a rush of gratitude. "I think she just likes the necklace. It's gorgeous, Chrissy. I've never seen one like it. And it's perfect for your dinner party."

Chrissy shrugged. "Maybe you're right." She turned back to Caroline. "You know, Cara," she said, "I do like that necklace. It looks nice on you, it's just a little funkier than what you normally wear. You usually look best in plain things."

"Plain things?" Caroline repeated, as if she wasn't quite sure she'd heard correctly. "I like classic things, but not *plain* things. I don't look dull, do I?"

"Of course not," Tracy assured her.

"No, you don't look dull," Chrissy added. "I just meant, uh, it's different from what you usually wear."

"That's just it," Cara said, grinning at Tracy. "It's time I changed my image. Actually, I wanted something, oh, something that you might wear, Chrissy. But not as wild as those earrings," she quickly added.

Chrissy's face fell, but she tried valiantly to hide it. "Well, I guess I'd wear the necklace," Chrissy said. "Yes, definitely, get the necklace. I think it will look great with your suit."

"Done!" Trying not to giggle, Caroline took the necklace to the cashier.

Afterwards, they strolled down Haight Street until they found a café that wasn't too crowded. As they were taking the first sips of their delicious coffee and chocolate capuccinos, Caroline slipped the necklace box out of her shoulder bag. She placed it on the table in front of Chrissy.

"You'd better take this now, before I forget," she said casually.

Chrissy looked up, startled. "Isn't that your new necklace

"*Your* new necklace," Caroline corrected.

"I don't get it," Chrissy said, obviously totally bewildered.

"I bought it for you," Caroline told her, pushing the box toward her cousin.

"She had it planned the whole time," Tracy blurted out. "As a surprise. It's to go with your new yellow silk. We nearly died when you wanted those earrings—they were completely wrong for it!" She burst into giggles at the surprised look on Chrissy's face.

"It was for me?"

"I wanted to do something nice for you," Caroline said quietly. "We haven't been getting along too great lately, and it's mostly my fault. And, besides, you have been a good sport about staying here this year, when you really didn't want to. And . . . and I just wanted you to know, I do care about what you're going through, and well . . ." Chrissy was staring so hard at her, Caroline stopped in confusion.

"Oh, Caroline, you are the best cousin a girl ever had!" Chrissy leaped across the table and threw her arms around Caroline's shoulders, hugging her so hard the both of them almost toppled onto the floor.

"Chrissy!" Embarrassed, Caroline burst out laughing.

"Oh, Cara—you are just so sweet! And here I was, thinking you were just jealous of me, when all along . . ." Chrissy hugged her again.

Tracy beamed at both of them. "Enough of this kiss and makeup," she joked. "People are staring."

"I'm sorry if I acted like a jerk," Chrissy told Caroline as she took her seat again.

Caroline smiled. "You weren't a jerk," she assured her cousin. "You were fine. I'm just glad you do like the necklace."

"Oh, I do!" Chrissy exclaimed.

"Why don't you try it on?" Tracy suggested. "Let's see how it looks."

Chrissy pulled the long strand of beads from the box and draped it over her sweater, wrapping it around several times. "How's that?"

"Pretty funky," Tracy said.

"Not bad," Caroline admitted. "You have the right touch."

When they walked home later, arm in arm, Caroline felt buoyantly happy.

This is more like it, she thought. *No more hard feelings—and that's the way I intend to keep things.*

"Chrissy," she said that night as they got ready for bed, "I have a great idea for the Activities Committee. How about a Senior Game Show that's also an academic contest? You could have semi-finals and then a big playoff, with prizes and everything. The teachers would like it too. What do you think?"

"Not bad," Chrissy said. "I'll propose it Wednesday at my breakfast meeting."

Caroline felt a burst of pride. If Chrissy took her up on the idea, it would be almost as good as being part of the committee. At last she would feel like she was really involved with things.

"You know, Cara," Chrissy said, "I really love heading this committee. I love being so busy. And I like getting other kids involved, too. I'm really sorry you decided to take acting lessons instead of helping me out with it. If you were there too, well, it would be just about perfect."

Chrissy was gazing at her so innocently from the other bed that Caroline didn't have the heart to tell her the truth—that she had wanted to be on the committee more than just about anything, but her injured pride had stopped her. No, there was no use in saying that now. Chrissy was so happy, it would ruin her good mood. And for the first time in weeks, Caroline was happy too.

Chapter 12

Sunday morning was as bright and beautiful as the day before had been foggy and dim, and Caroline woke up feeling extra energized. Glancing at the bed across the room she immediately saw that Chrissy was still sound asleep. There was nothing strange about that. Since Chrissy had arrived in San Francisco, she'd learned to sleep late on weekends, and often tried to sleep late on school days, too.

Chrissy sure has changed, Caroline thought, grinning to herself. *She used to rise at dawn until she realized she didn't have any chickens to feed here.*

Very quietly, so she wouldn't wake Chrissy, Cara rolled out of bed, poking her toes into her slippers. She grabbed a clean set of clothes and tiptoed down the hall to dress in the bathroom. She was in an extra-kind and considerate mood this morning.

I'm so glad Chrissy and I are getting along again,

she mused. *I think we both had fun last night—just like old times.*

As she finished dressing, Caroline suddenly stared at her image in the mirror. She looked neat and clean as usual, with her hair tied back smoothly in a ribbon. Grinning impishly, she yanked the ribbon around, tying a small, neat bow over one ear. Why hide the knot like she usually did? She felt a little dashing today, a little bit daring. Pleased with the effect, she entered the kitchen humming to herself.

"Someone's in a good mood." Her father grinned at her. Both her parents were already up and having breakfast together.

"Um—do I smell fresh coffee?" Caroline flashed them a dazzling smile.

"The best French Roast," her father said. "And the best fresh croissants in the world." He gestured at the table where a plateful of the delicious, buttery-rich rolls sat on a plate with slabs of butter and strawberry jam.

"That looks awfully good," Caroline's mouth watered.

"And we've got the house specialty—*Café au lait*," her father added. "Or hot chocolate, like your mother has."

"*Café au lait*, of course."

Her father loved to make coffee in the real French style, served in huge bowls with steamed milk, but he didn't often have the time, so it was a special treat. It was such fun to lift the steaming bowl between cupped hands and drink like a child—much more satisfying that balancing a cup with a delicate handle.

"Mmm. *Trés magnifique*," Caroline said, placing her bowl of coffee on the table, and pulling out the chair across from her mother.

"Here, honey." Her mother held out the bread plate. Caroline was about to accept a croissant, when she suddenly had a better idea. "On second thought," she said, "I've had an inspiration! I think I'll call Zach. I'm going to invite him to meet me out for breakfast."

"Oh? What's the occasion?" Her mother put down her bowl of hot chocolate.

"No occasion. It's just that, well, we didn't part on the best of terms last week, and I haven't seen him since." Caroline narrowed her eyes thoughtfully. "I don't want to let any bad feelings hang in the air."

Her parents exchanged amused glances. "Very wise," her father said.

Caroline smiled brightly. "Let's hope Zach thinks so," she bubbled.

Her mother laughed. "Cara, you're so cheerful! It's getting harder and harder to tell you and Chrissy apart. You're acting just like her."

"I am? How?" Caroline put down her bowl in surprise.

"Oh, you're so—enthusiastic. And optimistic."

"Not the staid, old Caroline, huh?"

"I didn't say that," her mother quickly protested.

Caroline sprang up to place her hands on her mother's shoulders. She gave them an affectionate squeeze. "I'm joking, Mom. It's okay. Just making fun of myself."

"That doesn't sound like you either."

"It doesn't sound like the *old* me," Caroline

corrected. "The new me is carefree and not so serious."

Her mother stared at Caroline's beaming face. "Well, this change in you is going to take a while to get used to, but I think I like it."

Caroline's father burst out laughing. "Me too."

Caroline grinned at her father. "Good." She leaned over for a gulp of coffee. "Well, I've got to make that phone call."

Zach answered the phone right away. At first, Caroline was relieved because she would have been nervous speaking to his parents, but Zach spoke so coldly to her she almost wished someone else had answered.

"Zach, I've been meaning to call you," Caroline began. "I—I should apologize."

"What for?" he asked warily.

"For letting you leave in such a bad mood last week."

"It wasn't your fault."

Caroline hesitated. "I shouldn't have let you go until we'd cleared things up between us."

"There's nothing to clear up," Zach said.

"Yes there is," Caroline insisted. "But I don't want to do it over the phone." She took a deep breath. This was almost like asking a boy for a date; and the old Caroline would have a terribly hard time doing that. But not the new Caroline, she reminded herself.

"Zach, can you meet me for breakfast? I know this great place. It's really punk—in a converted warehouse, all decorated with paintings and wild art. And," she continued, before Zach could refuse, "you can get a mountain of eggs and home fries and toast for almost nothing. How about meeting me?"

"I guess so. Sure, that sounds good," he agreed, and Caroline thought he sounded almost happy.

Beaming, Caroline explained how to get there, then she said a quick goodbye to her parents and hurried to the bus. Twenty minutes later, she was sitting at a table in Patsy's Place.

Maybe I hurried too much, she thought. *There's no sign of Zach yet.*

Caroline felt uncomfortable waiting alone in a bustling restaurant. She glanced anxiously around the room. There were lots of large groups of people and many couples, all eagerly chatting over rough wooden tables.

When the waiter passed by again, Caroline asked for a cup of coffee. Then she ordered herself to relax. By the time Zach finally appeared, she was feeling much better.

"Am I late?" He sat breathlessly across from her. "It took forever to get a bus."

"I didn't mind. I like to people-watch. Have some coffee before we order," she suggested.

"That's okay, I know what I want. The breakfast you described on the phone." Zach signaled the waiter and they both ordered the eggs and home fries.

"That ought to give us enough energy to rehearse today—if we want to," Caroline said. "I know we didn't plan a rehearsal . . ."

"I wasn't sure where we stood," Zach admitted.

"That's why we needed to talk. I shouldn't have let you leave in a huff last week."

"I wasn't in a huff," he protested.

"But you weren't in a good mood," Caroline said. She glanced at him quickly across the table. "I guess we both have artistic temperaments."

"That's me, all right." Zach smiled shyly.

Caroline smiled back and took another sip of her coffee. "No hard feelings?" she asked.

"No," Zach said, shaking his head, "of course not."

"Good. I can't stand being in a fight. It's funny, actually," Caroline mused. "I hate dramatics in my personal life. You'd think I wouldn't like acting. But I do."

"I'm the exact opposite," Zach admitted. "I fly off the handle pretty easily, I guess. I'll try to control my temper better, especially while we're working together."

"And I'll try to be more flexible."

Zach grinned at her as the waiter placed their breakfasts on the table. Feeling on top of the world, Caroline dug happily into her scrambled eggs.

Chapter 13

"Tracy! Wait up," Caroline called on Monday afternoon. She tried to push her way through the after-school crowd gathered at the main doors to Maxwell High. Tracy was a few yards ahead, and Caroline was dying to hear everything that happened with Tony Boyd that day. She had spotted him in the hall that morning, dressed in a brand new pullover and carefully pressed jeans. He looked especially cute, she thought, and wondered if he had dressed up for his 'date' with Tracy in the library.

All day, she had been excited for her best friend. Tracy hadn't gone out with anyone special since George Dietz—but that was several months ago. Caroline knew it was hard for Tracy, especially when Caroline had run into Luke in Hawaii. She could imagine how left out Tracy must have felt, though she'd never said a word.

So Caroline was especially glad for her friend now. If only she could reach her! She pushed her way clear of the crowd and called her name again. Then she spotted Chrissy up ahead. Chrissy and Tracy greeted each other like conspirators, huddling together, giggling and whispering. Cara suddenly stopped in her tracks. She felt like an intruder, and she didn't know what to do.

Don't be so silly. There's room enough for everyone in Tracy's life.

Annoyed at herself, she was about to rush ahead when Maria grabbed her elbow from behind.

"Cara! Am I glad to see you! Could you believe that pop quiz in history? I flunked, for sure."

"Maria, hi," Caroline said, pulling her arm free from Maria's grasp. "I'm trying to catch up with Tracy."

"Oh right! Today was her big 'date' with Tony Boyd! What happened?"

"I don't know—come on." She tried to drag Maria with her.

"Ouch, that hurt," Maria complained. "Tracy isn't there anyway."

Caroline stared. Maria was right—Tracy had disappeared. "Oh," she said in disappointment.

"But here comes Chrissy!" Maria exclaimed. She grabbed Chrissy's arm as Chrissy approached. "What happened? Did he ask her out? Does he like her?"

Chrissy grinned. "Holy mazoley, Maria. Hold your horses—I'll tell you everything."

"They are just the cutest couple," Maria raved. "*Are* they a couple?"

"Maybe." Chrissy grinned mysteriously.

"What happened?" Caroline asked impatiently. "Come on, Chrissy. Tell us."

"I feel like the cat who swallowed the canary," Chrissy joked. "I don't know if I should say. After all, it's personal. Between Tracy and Tony."

"Chrissy Madden, I'll kill you if you don't stop teasing and tell!" Maria was nearly beside herself.

Caroline was just as anxious to hear what happened. "Please, Chrissy," she pleaded, "what did Tracy say?"

Chrissy's smug grin grew bigger. "Okay. Tony was early. He was already waiting when Tracy got there."

"That's a good sign," Maria exclaimed.

"Then," Chrissy continued, "he sat very close to her. Of course, the table was kind of crowded. Everyone takes fifth period study hall in the library."

"We know that." Maria and Caroline groaned together.

Chrissy paused and Caroline could tell that she loved having them hang on her every word. "Well," she said dramatically, "they sat there—and nothing happened. I mean, they just studied."

"Oh no." Caroline and Maria exchanged disappointed looks.

"So, I thought I'd better do something—fast."

"You were there?" Caroline stared at Chrissy, aghast.

"I wasn't going to let her go through with it alone," Chrissy said calmly.

"I don't believe it," Maria squealed.

Caroline bit her lip. Tracy was *her* best friend. She should have been the one in the library! Of course, she hadn't even thought of it, but if she had, she never would have dreamed of interfering.

Why am I always so prim and proper? she wondered.

"So, what did you do," Maria prompted Chrissy.

"Well, I just happen to know . . ."

"She just happens to know. Hah!" Maria poked Caroline in the ribs, smirking.

"I just happen to know that Tony Boyd is a nut about model ships."

"You're kidding!"

"Nope." Chrissy smirked. "His great-grandfather was a sea captain. Sailed out of the Old Barbary Coast, right here in the city. Everyone in Tony's family is nuts about ships. They even have a collection of models—it's worth a small fortune." Chrissy paused, glancing at them importantly.

"How on earth did you find out?" Maria gaped in disbelief.

Caroline couldn't help grinning. "Are you kidding?" she asked. "Give Chrissy five minutes with anyone and she'll know their entire life's story." Caroline turned back to Chrissy. "But what do model ships have to do with anything?"

"Aha!" Chrissy's eyes lit up. "This is the best part. I knew something had to bring Tracy and Tony together, and the only thing I had to work with was model ships." She took a deep breath, and the words fairly exploded from her. "So—I rushed right over to their table, to tell Tracy I simply couldn't help her today. I said I'd have to come over some other day to help her finish the model ship she's making for her father's birthday!"

"Her father has model ships too?" Maria looked confused.

"He does now," Chrissy said. "Or he will, as soon as Tracy buys one at the model shop."

"But why would she do that?"

"Cripes, Maria, aren't you listening," Chrissy cried. "She needs it for her father's birthday."

"But I remember Tracy buying a shirt for her father's birthday about a month ago," Maria said in confusion.

"Tony doesn't know that," Chrissy pointed out. "And he took my bait faster than a hound trees a 'coon."

"You mean," Caroline said, "Tony offered to help Tracy finish this phantom model?"

"Exactly." Chrissy beamed at them.

"You are incredible," Caroline said in admiration. "In one day, you have Tony Boyd going over to Tracy's house to help with a model that doesn't exist, for a birthday that already was."

"Can you think of another way to get them together?" Chrissy challenged.

"Not me," Maria said.

"Or me," Caroline admitted. "I guess that's why Tracy ran out of here so quickly."

"Right," Chrissy said. "To get to the model shop fast. She has to have the thing started by the time Tony gets there."

"I have to hand it to you," Caroline said, "no one else would have thought of it, Chrissy. Only you."

That's for sure, Caroline thought. *I certainly blew it this time. Now I'm really out of things.*

"Going home, Cara?" Chrissy waited, her arms cradling her books, a satisfied smile on her face.

"Sure." Caroline forced herself to smile good-naturedly. "I should be near the phone. I'll bet Tracy calls the instant Tony leaves."

"I bet she will," Chrissy agreed.

They both turned and waved goodbye to Maria.

Chapter 14

"Where are my good cufflinks?" Caroline's father yelled down the hall. "You girls haven't seen them, have you?"

"No, Dad," Caroline yelled back patiently. It seemed like everyone was going slightly crazy. Her father and mother had been on edge all day and Chrissy had been nervously talking virtually non-stop since they got home from school.

For the third time, Caroline went down the hall and pounded on the bathroom door. "Chrissy—will you get out of there already?"

"Almost done," Chrissy yelled back.

"Cara—aren't you dressed yet?" Hands on hips, Mrs. Kirby confronted her in the hall.

"I would be, if Chrissy wasn't hogging the bathroom," she complained.

"What am I going to do with this family?" Caroline's mother, fully dressed in an elegant, black cocktail dress for the last hour, paced up and down the hall.

It must really be a big deal tonight, if Mom's this nervous. Chrissy is right, Caroline decided, *Mom must really want a job at Ms. Halloran's gallery. That's why she's so uptight. I'll have to be on my best behavior tonight.*

Finally, Chrissy was out of the shower. Caroline rushed through her own shower and put on her makeup faster than she ever had before. She felt as if she were running a race as she pulled the white silk suit out of the closet.

She had always loved its tailored, traditional look, but tonight she couldn't help wishing she had gotten something new. She glanced at Chrissy, who was already dressed and inspecting her yellow outfit in front of the mirror.

"You look wonderful, Chrissy. Your necklace is perfect!" The crystal beads sparkled against the pale yellow silk. "It's just beautiful. I love the flower clasp, don't you?"

"Sure. And you look super, Cara. Your pearls really make that outfit. You look so elegant." Chrissy sighed wistfully.

Caroline sighed also. "I guess so." She frowned at her reflection.

"Is something wrong?" Chrissy asked.

"Oh, I guess I'm just bored with this look." Turning away, Caroline adjusted the tucks in her skirt. She didn't want to sound unhappy or jealous of Chrissy's new things. Chrissy would only get upset, and they'd been getting along so well lately.

Chrissy was fidgeting with her beads, twisting them this way and that in front of the mirror.

"Cara—tell me the truth," she burst out. "Do you really like this necklace? Is it right for tonight?"

"Are you kidding? I love those beads! They're elegant and funky at the same time. They look great with this, or with your usual jeans . . ." The look on Chrissy's face told her she'd said the wrong thing.

"That's what I thought!" Chrissy plopped on the bed, sulking. "Everyone thinks I'm the jeans and sweatshirt type! I'm not! I can look elegant too, sometimes! Just once," she complained heatedly, "I'd like people to tell me I look sophisticated, like you. The best they ever say is I look funky."

Caroline stared at her cousin in shock. She would have been insulted, except she knew that Chrissy didn't mean it that way. "I'm sorry, Chrissy. I guess I shouldn't have bought them. I didn't mean to force them on you."

"And I didn't want to hurt your feelings. You were so sweet to get me a present. But what I really wanted for tonight was something really elegant— like your pearls." Chrissy sighed. "I could hardly ask Aunt Edith to buy me pearls. Especially when she already spent a bundle on me."

Pouting, Chrissy wriggled into her pillows, while Caroline resisted telling her not to wrinkle her silk clothes.

"Look, Chrissy," she said instead, "that necklace is dressier than you think. Here, I'll show you." Removing her pearl choker, Caroline reached for the crystal necklace. Chrissy handed it to her gladly.

Caroline draped the rope of beads over her head, wrapping it several times. The effect was perfect—a little wild and far out, but still very dressy. Very elegant. Exactly as she'd hoped it would look on Chrissy.

"You're wrong, Chrissy," she said. "These look fine!"

Chrissy squinted at her. "Cara—let me try your pearls on. Just for fun?"

"Well, okay." Caroline handed her the choker and helped Chrissy fasten the clasp.

Chrissy admired herself in the mirror. "That's more like it! Now I look understated and sophisticated—like you!"

Caroline frowned. It was hard to share her prized pearls—but she had to admit they looked fine on Chrissy. And she liked the way she looked in the crystal beads. Suddenly, she giggled.

"Chrissy—wouldn't it be funny if we wanted to dress like each other—just for a change?"

"I think you're right," Chrissy exclaimed. "I want to be sophisticated for once, and you want to look funky!"

"We're usually so different. It's hard to believe you want to look like me," Caroline said. "But I am tired of being so predictable. And if I don't watch out, I could get—boring."

Chrissy shook her head in disbelief. "When I first came here, I thought you were the most elegant, self-possessed girl in the world. I almost died! Your clothes were always perfect, you're incredibly graceful, plus you speak French and know all about foods I'd never even heard of. I was terrified of acting like a geek around you."

"*Mon Dieu*, Chrissy." Caroline flushed. "You're embarrassing me."

"But it's true," Chrissy went on. "I was all cowboy boots, bandanas, and Iowa slang." She frowned. "You thought I was a real country bumpkin—admit it."

"But not anymore," Caroline confessed, a little embarrassed. Grabbing Chrissy's shoulders, she pivoted her toward the mirror. "Look—with my pearls on, you're as understated and elegant as anyone."

"You really think so?"

"Absolutely. Here." Caroline unfastened her pearl stud earrings. "Wear the pearls tonight, and take these—they're perfect with it."

"I love it!" Excitedly, Chrissy fastened the earrings on, beaming at herself in the mirror.

"I'll wear plain gold hoops," Caroline decided, going to her jewelry box. "They'll be just the right touch, with this wild necklace."

"You're really going to wear it?"

"Absolutely. Oh—but they're still your beads, Chrissy."

"Okay, but you can wear them anytime you want," Chrissy said generously.

"Great!" Caroline admired her new style. The crystal beads jazzed up her whole look so that the things she'd had for ages—the suit and the gold hoop earrings—looked brand new.

"Golly, Caroline—you look positively funky! It's—it's a major breakthrough!"

Her mother's voice cut through the air. "Are you girls ever coming? We're late!"

"Ready, Mom." Caroline stole one last glance at the mirror. She looked exactly the way she'd hoped.

This old suit worked out after all! It's like the best of me and Chrissy combined—something classic and formal and something new and casual. Chrissy's right—it is a breakthrough. And I love it!

As they paraded down the hall for inspection, her mother looked up, startled. "Why, you're perfectly beautiful! Both of you." She hugged Caroline and Chrissy in turn. "I'll be extra proud of my family tonight."

Chrissy and Caroline exchanged pleased glances.

"I called for a cab," her mother said hurriedly. "They'll be here any minute so I'm going down to wait on the porch. Hurry, everyone."

Chrissy grabbed her good coat. "I told you," she whispered, nudging Caroline, "your mom's really after this job." She hurried down the stairs to the porch.

Caroline grabbed her father's arm. "Dad—Chrissy has this silly idea that Mom wants a job with Ms. Halloran. Is it true?"

"A new job?" Her father cleared his throat—what he always did when he was being evasive. "Well, your mother has talked a lot about Ms. Halloran's gallery lately, and I know they are negotiating some kind of deal, but a new job?" Musing, he slipped his arms into his raincoat. "She never said anything to me about it, but I do know tonight is important to her. So, be on your absolutely best behavior."

"I know," Caroline sighed. "I know."

Actually, the night turned out to be a total bore, as far as Caroline was concerned. Except for the pleasure of receiving compliments on her outfit, her worst fears were confirmed.

It was just as she'd told Chrissy—the gallery was so crowded you couldn't see the art, just a crush of people trying not to spill drinks on each other. The whole reception felt interminable and the formal dinner was even worse. She and Chrissy were seated at a separate little table as if they were children, and seated so far down at the opposite end of the room that they only had each other to talk to. Caroline felt insulted, and she only hoped her mother was happy with the evening; every time she spotted her, Ms. Halloran had her cornered. They seemed to have an awful lot to talk about.

"This is a real drag," Chrissy announced as dessert was finally served. "You should have warned me it was going to be boring."

"I did warn you," Caroline pointed out.

"What a waste of a new dress," Chrissy complained.

"At least we'll be home fairly early. In case you're worried about getting up on time tomorrow."

"Why would I worry about that?"

"Your breakfast meeting—or did you forget?"

"I didn't forget," Chrissy said innocently, "but since I've been half-asleep all evening, I could stay up as late as I want."

"You're incredible," Caroline laughed.

Chrissy waved her blueberry muffin in the air. "This meeting will now come to order!"

"I second the motion," Tracy giggled, lifting her buttered toast.

Caroline grinned. Only Chrissy could get away with a meeting like this—everyone clowning around, but still getting down to business. She was glad she'd decided to join them at the last minute.

Obviously, Tracy felt the same way. "This is a wild committee meeting," she whispered to Caroline. "I only came because I owed it to Chrissy, for getting me together with Tony."

"I take it the model ship is a big success?"

"Completely," Tracy said.

"Has he asked you out yet?"

"No—but he will."

Up in the front of the room Chrissy cleared her throat importantly. "The first order of the day is new ideas for class activities."

Caroline stood, raising her hand politely.

"The chair recognizes Caroline Kirby," Chrissy said formally. "With a great idea—a Senior Game Show!"

"Chrissy—I'm supposed to tell," Caroline chided her. "Anyway, Chrissy's right. I thought we could combine academics with fun. Really go all out with the game show theme." Excitedly, Caroline described her idea to the other seven committee members.

"We'd have an announcer and a couple of hosts and hostesses to lead contestants onto the stage. And we could hold up cue cards for the audience, to applaud and hiss and boo and things like that." She paused to take a breath and Chrissy nodded at her encouragingly.

"But the questions would be serious—and tough. Fitting good old Maxwell High's image. So—what do you think?"

Bill Rice gulped down a mouthful of food. "But

Skit Night's in the fall. It's always been that way. We can't do a dumb game show."

Caroline's cheeks grew hot. "If you like the idea, we could. There's no law that says Skit Night has to be first."

"Maybe Bill's right," Chrissy said, "if fall's always been the time for Skit Night. Everyone looks forward to it." She banged her coffee mug on the desk like a gavel. "I think this year's skits should have a common theme."

"Like what?" Bill asked.

"How about the movies?" Chrissy leaned forward eagerly. "All the skits could be movie satires."

Cheeks burning, Caroline tried to sit down without looking as foolish as she felt. Around her, everyone was talking at once, discussing possible themes for skit night. Trying not to let the others see how upset she was, Caroline stirred milk into her coffee, keeping her head down.

Chrissy was going on about the important role the emcee played on skit night.

"It's really critical," she went on. "We have to get someone who's a good actor, because a good actor can carry the whole show—right Cara?"

Startled, Caroline pulled herself together. "Uh, right, I guess. A good actor, or actress, can set the tone of an evening."

"That's what I meant," Chrissy exclaimed, giving Caroline a pleased smile. "And Cara should know— she's taking a professional acting workshop this year. She knows what a good emcee can mean to a show—its success or failure."

She gave Caroline a meaningful look.

She means me, Caroline realized. *She let them*

shoot down my game show idea because she knows I could do the best job as emcee! After all, I'm the only one in the class taking acting lessons.

Gratefully, Caroline returned Chrissy's look, nodding as if to tell her she understood perfectly. Chrissy winked.

"Since I agree so strongly with Cara," Chrissy told the group, "I think we should set a new tradition. Usually, the class president has been emcee, but that doesn't always make for a good show."

"That's true," Tracy commented. "Last year, Eve Franklin did a terrible job. Boring!"

Everyone groaned in agreement.

"What do you suggest?" Bill asked Chrissy.

"Auditions. Like for a regular performance. After all, that's what Skit Night is—a performance. And if word gets out that the emcee is funny and the show is good, attendance will be up over last year. That's better for class spirit."

"She's right," Ellen said. "We should hold auditions. Only someone really professional should be emcee."

Caroline sat back, biting her lip in anticipation. Auditions! She always did well at them, ever since her days in ballet class. She could just see herself as emcee.

I know I can do a good job! And the best part is— I'll feel like part of my class—at last! This is the chance I've been waiting for. I don't mind anything now—I'm even glad I'm not on the committee!

She couldn't wait to discuss it with Zach. With his advice and a few special acting techniques, Caroline knew she could be the best emcee Maxwell High ever saw!

Chapter 15

Caroline entered the auditorium, nervous, but confident. After hours on the phone with Zach the night before outlining strategies and techniques she knew she'd get the job. Zach had a million ideas. He knew more about acting than Caroline had ever dreamed there was to it.

Glancing at her note cards, she took a deep breath. He had dictated what seemed like hundreds of jokes; too many to memorize, but she had to have them all on hand. She didn't know which joke might feel right when she was actually performing. She had jokes to begin with, jokes to end with, jokes to use on hecklers, and jokes to use when other jokes fell flat. Caroline never felt like an especially funny person, but Zach had given her such a pep talk, that she was sure his techniques would carry her through. They were guaranteed to

make her funny, Zach had said. Nervous as she
was, she couldn't wait for a chance to try them all
out. Zach would be so proud of her when she got
the part. And for herself it would make up for
missing out on other things.

Hastily, she glanced around the crowded auditorium. She spotted Maria sitting with Justine and
Randy and slid into a seat next to her.

"Is everyone here to audition for emcee?" She
was surprised at the number of people who had
stayed after school for the auditions.

"Not everyone, I hope," Justine answered, "or
we'll be here until tomorrow. We're just here to
watch."

"Yeah, I thought I might hear some good jokes
that I can use later," Randy added.

Maria winked at Caroline. "Well, we all know
how old your jokes are Randy. I think they've been
passed down through the centuries."

The girls all laughed, especially when Randy
scrunched his face in mock anger.

"Well thank you very much, Maria," he said. "As a
matter of fact, my great, great, great, great-grandfather was a stand-up comedian in the old country."

"What did he stand up on?" Justine asked in an
innocent voice. This time even Randy had to laugh.

"These auditions had better be funny," Randy
said. "We're a tough audience. If we don't laugh,
they're out."

"Chrissy said she really wants someone lively
and funny, to make sure Skit Night isn't a bore,"
Justine added.

"Like last year's," Randy groaned. "Bor-ring! Half
the audience fell asleep."

"It was pretty bad," Justine agreed.

"She had terrible material," Maria added. "Some of those skits were really lame, and people acted like it was her fault! All she did was introduce the acts."

"Yeah, but that's half the battle," Randy insisted. "If she was funny, the skits would seem funnier."

"That's not true. That has nothing to do with it," Justine said hotly.

"Oh no?" Randy gave her a superior look. "It's like the Johnny Carson Show. His guests can bomb, but the show is still funny because of the jokes he makes about them bombing."

Justine crossed her arms stubbornly. "Maybe, but I'm not convinced. I still think that it will be the skits that make the show."

"Cara, what do you think?" Randy sat forward.

Caroline had been holding her tongue, afraid to sound like she was showing off. "Actually, I agree with Randy. The emcee is crucial. He sets the tone for the whole evening. If the emcee is entertaining, then everyone has a good time, no matter what."

"Right!" Triumphantly, Randy sat back.

"I think he paid you to say that," Maria cracked.

Justine eyed Caroline carefully. "I think someone here wants to be emcee."

"Do you?" Now Maria and Randy looked at her curiously.

Caroline fiddled self-consciously with the strap of her purse. "I thought you all knew," she said.

"Why would we?" Maria demanded.

"Didn't Chrissy mention it? Or Tracy—she was at the meeting."

"What meeting?"

"Never mind," Caroline said. "It doesn't matter. I am trying out to be emcee. I figure my acting class will be a big help, and I should have a good chance at it."

"Whoa—tough talk." Randy grinned, impressed, and Caroline blushed.

"Well, I am pretty confident," she said modestly.

"You're the chairperson's cousin," Justine remarked. "That won't hurt you."

Caroline blushed even redder. "I intend to win on my talent. Anyway," she added to change the subject, "who's my competition?"

"It's rough," Maria answered. "Connie Willis is hot for the part—and she's pretty funny. So is Bob Freedlander."

"Yeah, but Chrissy's sure to put in a good word for Cara," Randy said knowingly. "They'll never get it. Cara's in for sure."

"Don't be so fast," Caroline said quickly. "Chrissy is only one member of the committee. And she won't play favorites. I've got to really be good up there."

"Well, I know you will be," Maria said warmly. "When you set out to do something, Cara, you do it. I've seen you in action. Plus, you're a great performer."

"Thanks." Caroline could have hugged Maria for the vote of confidence.

Onstage, Chrissy and her committee members were conferring with Mr. Wells, the activities adviser. As he rose to the microphone and called for quiet, Caroline felt a burst of energy—they were ready to begin! All around her, the spectators settled down, ready to be entertained. Mr. Wells introduced Chrissy, who strode confidently to the microphone at the center of the stage.

"Hi, everybody! We're all here to audition an emcee for Senior Skit Night. We're looking for someone to personally prevent Senior Slump."

She went on, saying how important activities like this were to the spirit of this last and crucial year. Caroline was only half listening. Bob and Connie, several rows in front of her, both seemed as nervous and eager as she was. Caroline craned her neck, scanning the large auditorium, but didn't see any sign of Tracy.

I hope she's coming! I need her to root for me especially hard, Caroline thought, a sudden grip of fear enveloping her.

Chrissy ended her remarks. "Enough from me. I know you're all dying to hear the excruciatingly funny remarks of our fellow classmates and would-be Senior Skit Night emcees—so without further ado . . ." She glanced at the list in her hand, "Here's Connie Willis."

Nervously, Connie rose. Taking off the glasses she usually wore, she rushed up the few steps to the stage, but at the top, she lost her balance, stumbling badly. With a cry of dismay, she tripped and fell forward with a thud. Some kids in the audience gasped, and Mr. Wells rushed to help, but it was obvious Connie wasn't hurt—except for her pride. Her face shone a fiery red as she stood up and waved away Mr. Wells. Caroline felt embarrassed for Connie. If she had taken a fall like that, she was sure she would have fled the auditorium, but Connie brushed herself off and headed toward center stage.

"Oops—have a nice trip, Connie?" Chrissy joked to the audience.

Everyone groaned. "Sorry folks—I'm not a stand-up comedian," Chrissy grinned, "and neither is Connie, from the looks of it. But I do hope she's okay."

"I am, thanks." With an abashed smile, Connie shared the microphone with Chrissy.

"Seriously," Chrissy said, "let's give her a round of applause."

"I might not get one *after* my jokes," Connie said.

Everyone applauded loudly.

"Chrissy sure handled that well," Maria murmured.

"Yeah—maybe she should be emcee," Randy suggested.

"She doesn't want the job," Caroline told him firmly. *This time I'm going to get it,* she thought, sitting back to hear what Connie had to say.

Connie's introductory speech fell flat, and Caroline could sense the audience's attention drifting away. But her jokes were good.

"When she sticks to the funny stuff, she's great," Justine commented.

"I agree," Caroline said. "She is terribly funny."

"That's not enough," Maria said thoughtfully. "She has to be sincere too—and able to get the audience involved. I wouldn't vote for her."

"Then don't applaud," Randy told her. "That's how the committee will know we're not behind her."

Caroline felt funny, not applauding. Any performer deserved a hand, she thought. But if Chrissy and the others were to judge from the audience's reaction, it was important not to be *too* enthusiastic. The applause for Connie was polite, but not wild.

Bob was next, and as expected, they were all treated to a few minutes of helpless laughter as Bob cracked joke after joke.

"He's just like Connie," Maria whispered. "Funny—but no warmth. We need someone with class spirit, too."

Then it was Caroline's turn. She could hardly believe she was moving so calmly toward the stage as Chrissy announced her name. She made it up the steps smoothly.

Don't be nervous. There's no reason to be scared, she assured herself. *I've got great material.*

Caroline told her opening joke, which was received with loud guffaws of laughter. She started to tell her next joke, when she suddenly realized that she was making the same mistake Connie and Bob had made. While her jokes were funny, she sounded detached. Her routine needed a personal touch. Mid-sentence, she stopped and looked straight into the audience.

"I can't help thinking," she said slowly, "that there's more to Skit Night than laughter. There's also the closeness with our classmates, and the sadness of knowing that this is our last year together. We've been through a lot—all of us and Maxwell High. Some good, and some bad, but all things we'll never forget, not for the rest of our lives."

She felt the audience hanging on her words.

They're moved—and so am I. I really mean what I'm saying, she thought.

"I just want to say, that . . ."

Suddenly Chrissy was standing at the microphone beside her.

"Cara's right!" Her eyes were shining the way they did when Chrissy got excited. "I don't mean to steal Cara's spotlight, but I've got something to add and I'm sure she won't mind. This school is made of memories, for all of us. I remember when I first came here. I felt pretty alone. This place is huge, and there are so many different kinds of people here!" The audience was silent, listening hard, while Caroline simply stared at her cousin without saying a word. Chrissy continued her impromptu speech. "I know I'm not very sophisticated or worldly—but I've been awfully lucky! I had my cousin, Cara, who made all the difference in the world."

There was a cheer from the audience.

"And a bunch of friends who can't be beat."

There was more cheering and some applause.

"The thing is," Chrissy went on, growing more and more animated, "once I started meeting people, I found out that even though we're all different on the outside, we're all pretty much the same inside."

The audience was still again, moved by what she was saying.

"And," Chrissy told them, "when I had some . . . personal troubles, recently, you all were so good to me. So supportive—well, what I really mean is, that's what makes a good senior class—good hearted souls—people willing to go an extra mile for a friend. People you can count on."

There were even more cheers and applause.

Feeling foolish and forgotten, Caroline stood behind Chrissy. Awkwardly, she smiled and applauded along with everyone else, feeling smaller by the minute.

What is going on? she wondered. *Chrissy is stealing the show. No one even remembers I'm up here! And I can hardly tell more jokes after her heart-rending speech!*

She felt her smile grow stiff and fixed on her face. Her body felt rigid. She didn't know what to do. Should she stay where she was, or sit down? Sitting down would draw even more attention to herself, so she decided to back up against the curtains, staying out of Chrissy's way, but not disappearing altogether.

Scanning the animated audience, she noticed that Tracy had slipped in. She was alone—did that mean things weren't going well with Tony Boyd? As far as Caroline knew, he still hadn't asked her out, but Tracy was still waiting hopefully.

Caroline was staring straight at Tracy, trying to get her attention, when she was startled by a loud burst of applause.

Mr. Wells must have seen her confusion. Leaning over, he whispered to her, "Josh just nominated Chrissy for emcee."

"Chrissy?" Caroline gaped. In front of her, Chrissy was bowing and laughing while people applauded wildly, calling her name.

Numbly, Caroline stared up at Mr. Wells. "But, but I don't get it," she stammered. She held up the notes in her hand. "I mean, Chrissy isn't prepared. She hasn't written a speech or anything."

Part of Caroline's mind was thinking she would

still win—and she didn't want to hurt Chrissy's feelings. The other part was dimly aware that something awful was happening.

Chrissy stood close to the microphone, holding her hands up for quiet. "We have lots of fine people auditioning for emcee," she protested, but a chant started up. Caroline couldn't believe her eyes and ears—the whole room was full of people clapping and stamping their feet.

"We want Chrissy. We want Chrissy," they said at first. Then someone changed the words, making up a rhyme:

"Chris-sy for MC! Chris-sy for MC!"

Caroline felt the rhythm of the chant, pounding and thumping, as if it were pounding in her head. She pressed her hands against her temples.

Shrugging helplessly, Chrissy's smile spread from ear to ear. "Holy mazoley, guys—what can I say?" The audience stamped and whistled.

Flushed with pleasure, Chrissy turned to Caroline. "Jeepers, I don't believe it! What should I do, Cara?"

Caroline gave her a weak smile. "I don't know. It's up to you."

Chrissy flashed a wide happy grin at Mr. Wells, Josh, and the rest of the committee, then at the audience.

"Well, okay then," she said into the microphone, "I may be making a big mistake, but if you want me this much, well—I'll be proud to be emcee."

The audience broke out into rowdy applause. Caroline stepped to the side and managed to slip past Mr. Wells. Pressed close to the wall, she tiptoed down the stage steps. If she was an actress at all, she was acting now, trying to hide her feelings. All she wanted was to run as far away from the auditorium as she could go! But she'd left her purse and her books under her seat, next to Maria and the others. Picking her way back there now, she wished she could dissolve into thin air instead.

When she reached her chair, she dropped into it and bent down to gather her things together, grateful that her face was hidden. She was sure disappointment and shock were written all over it.

Maria bent down close to her to speak in her ear. "Cara—I'm sorry you didn't get to be emcee."

"Um, that's okay." Caroline shrugged.

"I didn't even think Chrissy wanted to be emcee."

"I know," Caroline said weakly. "She never mentioned it."

"Maybe she doesn't really want to do it," Maria said. "Maybe she'll change her mind when the fuss dies down."

"Are you crazy?" Justine leaned toward them, grinning widely. "Of course she wants to. She'd be perfect! I don't know why I didn't think of it myself."

"I certainly never thought of it," Caroline muttered. No one heard her.

Chrissy had launched into an elaborate acceptance speech, thanking nearly everyone she knew in San Francisco for the honor of being Senior Skit Night emcee.

Caroline nudged Maria. "Listen, I've got to go. Uh—I have a rehearsal, with my friend Zach. Congratulate Chrissy—if you see her before I do."

"Why don't you stay," Maria urged. "We'll all celebrate together?"

But Caroline was already halfway up the aisle.

Chapter 16

Caroline hurried toward the door. All she could hear was the roar of applause for Chrissy thundering through the auditorium.

I can't stand it! I really can't stand it! she thought.

She was painfully aware of all the people around her—friends and teachers, all clapping for Chrissy. How would it look if she ran from the room, abandoning Chrissy? What would people say?

For once, she decided, *I'm not going to worry about that. I've just got to get out of here.* Obeying her instinct, she ran blindly out of the auditorium and out of the school. On the street, she caught the first cable car going by.

Streets passed in a blur. Hardly knowing what she was doing, she decided to get off and start walking. Her mind was in a state of confusion, her thoughts tumbling wildly. When she found herself in front of the Bergdorf Acting Studio, she stopped in surprise.

She hadn't really meant to go there. She'd only made up the rehearsal with Zach as an excuse to get away. Then she remembered—Zach had said something about going to the library at the Studio today. In fact, he had told her to call him there if there was news about her audition.

There's news all right. But not what Zach expects, Caroline thought.

Pushing open the library door, she didn't have to look far to find Zach. He was there, right up front, near the door.

"Caroline!" He looked up with a welcoming smile. "I thought you'd call—you didn't need to come over here. You have news? The audition . . ."

"I . . . I didn't mean to come over. I just . . ." She burst into tears.

"Oh no," Zach said, "that bad?"

Caroline sank onto a chair. She nodded, grateful that she could at least count on Zach.

"People are staring." She tried to dry her eyes.

"They understand," Zach smoothed. "They've had bad auditions too."

"Oh, Zach—it's not just that." Caroline felt embarrassed all over again, thinking about the audition. "This sure is my day for public humiliation."

Zach smiled kindly. "I guess you lost, huh?"

Caroline shook her head. "Not exactly. Can we go somewhere to talk?"

"Follow me," he said. "We'll find an empty classroom."

Caroline followed him down the hall. Her tears seemed to keep coming, no matter how hard she tried to stop them.

"I—I told them I was coming here, to rehearse with you," she stammered as they entered a small room with a makeshift stage at one end. The room was deserted.

Zach sat on the edge of the stage and motioned for Caroline to sit next to him. "Told who?" he asked.

"My friends at school." She drew a deep breath and swallowed hard. "Oh, Zach—it was so awful. The worst day of my life."

"But what went wrong? Those jokes were good."

"I didn't tell the jokes! I never got a chance! Zach, I never auditioned at all."

"I don't get it."

Shakily, she explained what had happened, how she had tried to go with the mood of the crowd.

"And then Chrissy took over and gave a speech. I ended up just standing there, while they clapped and shouted for Chrissy. I felt like an idiot." Again, she swallowed hard. "They forgot all about me."

"Poor Caroline," Zach said softly.

"No, poor Chrissy," Caroline burst out. "That's all I ever hear anymore. Poor, poor Chrissy. Let's be extra-nice to Chrissy, let's make it up to her! And meanwhile, I get shoved aside."

Zach put his hand on Caroline's in a friendly gesture. "That must be tough."

"You bet it's tough! I could have done that audition. I was at least as good as Bob or Connie. I could have gotten the part."

Zach furrowed his brow. "Who are Bob and Connie?"

"Kids who auditioned before me. Before Chrissy got into the act."

"Did one of them get the part?" Zach asked. "I'm confused."

Caroline laughed bitterly. "They didn't stand a chance. Chrissy got the part, Zach."

"Chrissy! But she wasn't even auditioning to be emcee, was she?"

"No, but the place went wild for her."

Zach whistled. "Now I see why you're upset."

"Zach, I can't take any more of this!" Caroline cried. "If I hear one more word about poor Chrissy—I don't know what I'll do!"

They were silent for a moment, then they heard someone pounding on the door.

"Can I come in?" Uncertainly, Chrissy entered the room.

"Chrissy!" Caroline flushed. "What are you doing here?"

Chrissy hesitated. "You said you were rehearsing with Zach. I called home, but no one answered, so I thought I'd look for you here."

"Why?" Caroline glared at her cousin. "What do you need me for?"

"Well, I—I wanted to make sure you're okay."

Hastily, Caroline wiped her eyes, throwing her head back and straightening her shoulders. "Of course I'm okay. Why wouldn't I be."

"I don't know." Chrissy played with the string on her cotton jacket. "I thought that you might be upset. You didn't look very happy up on stage when everyone asked me to be emcee. I was afraid you might run away or something."

Caroline laughed. "Don't be ridiculous. I would never do anything so dumb."

"I know." Chrissy shrugged helplessly. "I don't know why I came here."

"Well, I'm not going anywhere," Caroline declared. "I'm sorry if that spoils your plans."

"But I don't want you to go anywhere, Cara," Chrissy said softly.

"Don't you?" Biting her lip, Caroline looked away.

"Maybe I should leave," Zach said, making a move to get up. "This is between the two of you."

"You can stay," Caroline told him. "You already know what's going on, anyway."

Zach squeezed her shoulder gently. "I'll wait in the library," he said. He walked to the door, then stopped to give Caroline a sympathetic smile before shutting it quietly behind him.

"Well, why don't you tell *me* what's going on?" Chrissy asked. She folded her arms across her chest and took a seat opposite the stage. "I don't see what the problem is."

"Oh no?" Caroline forced herself to speak calmly. "You stole my part, Chrissy. That's what the problem is."

"I couldn't do anything about that, Cara. Really I couldn't."

"You could have insisted on a proper audition."

"But they wanted me." Chrissy looked imploringly at her cousin, but Caroline wouldn't meet her eyes.

"But you could have thanked them and still said no," Caroline cried. "You could have said you didn't deserve it."

"But I did deserve it," Chrissy said innocently. "I have school spirit. I worked for the class . . ."

Caroline flung her hands over her ears. "Stop! I won't listen any more!"

"But it wasn't my fault," Chrissy insisted. "It's not like I planned it this way."

"You didn't try to stop it." Bitterly, Caroline poured out all her hurt feelings. "Everyone feels so sorry for you. You and your tragic tornado."

"I didn't cause the tornado," Chrissy protested.

"No—but you used it. You played on everyone's sympathy to get your own way."

"I did not!" Chrissy shouted, jumping out of her seat. "Take that back!" she demanded.

"No, Chrissy. Ever since it happened, you've been impossible to live with. You really feel sorry for yourself."

"You would too," Chrissy cried. "But I never asked anyone for pity."

"You didn't have to. They all bent over backwards for you."

"I think you're just jealous," Chrissy said stubbornly, taking her seat again. "You're angry because you're not emcee."

"It's more than that," Caroline said calmly. "It's everything that's happened ever since school started."

"I don't remember anything else."

"What about Mt. Tamalpais?"

Chrissy shrugged and frowned in confusion. "What about it? We had a great time. So what?"

"Don't you remember?" Caroline couldn't believe that Chrissy didn't know what she was talking about. "We were supposed to bring the desserts. Only you forgot them."

"No one cared."

"They cared when they thought I forgot," Caroline said quietly. "They came down hard on me until they found out you were the one who forgot. Then it was 'oh, it doesn't matter. We didn't want dessert anyway.'" Caroline mimicked her friends in a sarcastic tone of voice.

Chrissy colored. "But that's such a little thing. You're not still mad about that!"

"Then how about the committee? That was a big thing. I wanted to head that committee more than anything. I thought, finally, it was my day in the spotlight! My day to really belong at Maxwell High! I've lived here all my life, Chrissy, but that was my first chance to really be part of things. Then you came along, and everyone said, 'oh, poor Chrissy, she's so upset, let's make her chairperson.' They didn't even vote on it!"

Chrissy bit her lip. "Well, that wasn't my fault either," she defended herself. "They asked me to do it, you admit that yourself."

"And you didn't care how much it hurt me," Caroline said.

"I didn't know! What was I supposed to do? Turn it down?"

"Yes," Caroline cried. "It wasn't a fair way to get the job."

"Golly, Cara, I wanted to do it too. And I'm pretty good at it." Chrissy took a deep breath. "I think you're overreacting. I think you're taking a few little incidents and blowing them all out of proportion."

"It's more than a few," Caroline said. "There was also the new dress Mom bought you, and the necklace that I bought you that you didn't even like!" She paused. "But that's not even important compared to the way you tried to take Tracy away from me."

Chrissy gaped at her. "Tracy is *your* best friend. Everyone knows that."

"She *was.*" Tears spilled from Caroline's eyes. "Until you came along, with your scheme to get her together with Tony. I hardly see Tracy now—it's the two of you," she choked, "and I'm left out!"

Chrissy looked stricken. "Tracy's still your friend," she insisted. "I'm not trying to cut you out."

Head in hands, Caroline began to cry harder. She took a deep shaky breath and lifted her head to look at Chrissy, who was sitting quietly in the chair in front of her. In place of Chrissy's normally happy smile was a tight worried expression. "And what about my mother?" Caroline asked.

Bewildered, Chrissy shrugged. "What about her?"

"Mom told you all about that job at Ms. Halloran's gallery. Why didn't she tell me? Has she forgotten I exist?" Caroline's shoulders shook. "The only thing I had left was this audition—and you even took that away from me."

Uncomfortably, Chrissy shifted her weight. "I'm sorry, Cara. I . . . I didn't realize."

"You should have," she whispered. "You really hurt me, Chrissy. You let me down. Remember how you raved about my quiz show idea? But then, at the breakfast meeting, you acted like it was completely stupid, in front of everyone! I felt like an idiot. Why didn't you stick up for me, Chrissy? Why did you shoot me down?"

Chrissy frowned. "Everyone agreed that Skit Night was more important."

"But I should be important." Caroline's voice was rough and scratchy. "And the worst thing," she managed to say, "was today. You took the emcee job away from me. You shot me down again."

Weakly, Chrissy smiled. "Maybe you need a bullet proof vest," she joked.

Caroline gaped at her. "How can you laugh at me?" Her eyes flashed angrily. "How can you, Chrissy? I think you did it all on purpose! You wanted me to lose," she accused. "You want everything for yourself—my parts, my friends, everything! I think you're deliberately trying to ruin my senior year!"

"I am not."

"I wish you'd never come here," Caroline said heatedly. "I wish you'd go away—and leave me alone! I hate you, Chrissy Madden. I—I hate you for ruining my life!"

Chrissy turned pale. Caroline stared at her in stunned horror.

"Oh, Chrissy," she gasped. "I didn't mean that! Chrissy!"

But Chrissy had run from the room.

Chapter 17

Caroline sprang to the door and ran into the hall. Chrissy was halfway out the exit already.

"Chrissy, wait," she started to call, but the words died away in her throat. She leaned against the door frame.

"Well," Zach said from behind her, "aren't you going after her?"

Caroline hesitated. "I don't know."

"You started to."

"I know. Instinct, I guess." She frowned. "I think I'm too mad to talk right now. I mean, what she did to me was terrible!"

"I guess so." Zach shrugged. "But at least she followed you here."

"That's just because she has a guilty conscience. And she should." Just remembering what had happened that afternoon in the auditorium made Caroline's cheeks flame. "Chrissy humiliated me," she said.

"I know."

"We're not going to make up this time, either. I'll never forgive Chrissy for this. Never."

Zach rolled his eyes. "I'll believe that when I see it."

"Believe it. I've had enough. I can't take any more of this," Caroline said heatedly.

"Okay, okay, I believe you," Zach protested. "Don't yell at me, too."

"She really has a nerve," Caroline fumed, not listening to Zach. "She ruins my audition, and then she comes over here. For what? To run away? She sure didn't come here to apologize. She just came to gloat. How can she be so mean?"

Zach sat down. "So let me get this straight. You're not going after her?"

"Why should I?" Caroline burst out. "I'm tired of being the reasonable one. I can be angry. I have a right to be angry."

"No one said you didn't."

"Fine. Good." Caroline crossed her arms over her chest and glared at Zach. "She's the one who should be sorry. She's the one who owes me an apology. That hasn't changed." Caroline set her jaw. "But even if she does apologize, I'll never forgive her for this. Never."

Zach glanced at his watch and smiled uneasily. "Uh—I hate to interrupt, but I'm starved. Would it be all right if I went home now? I'd hate to miss dinner."

"Is it that late?" Caroline checked her watch, too. "Of course you can go, Zach. I didn't mean to give you a hard time." She sighed deeply. "You know, you're the only friend I've got left. I'm sorry I yelled at you."

"That's okay. Good luck at home."

"Thanks. I have a feeling I'll need it."

For a minute or two after Zach had left, Caroline sat staring at the walls. It was getting late. If she stayed much longer, she'd miss dinner. The last thing she needed was a family scene about that, on top of everything else.

When she left the building the sky had clouded over, and it looked like it was going to rain any second. *How appropriate,* thought Caroline. She considered going after Zach, to ask if she could have dinner at his house. She would do anything to avoid facing Chrissy right now. But that was stupid: she had to face her cousin sometime. After what seemed an eternity, the cable car came and she climbed on. For once, she wished San Francisco was an even larger city. It would give her more time to prepare herself for what would probably be a showdown. But as it was, she was home much too soon.

Cautiously, Caroline stuck her head in the front door. The apartment was quiet. Nearly on tiptoes, she made her way down the hall to the kitchen. She peered inside. Perfect—it was empty.

With a sigh of relief she dropped her books onto the counter and fetched the pitcher of iced tea from the refrigerator. Chrissy was probably in the bedroom blasting the stereo, as usual. Well, she would just hide out in the kitchen and pretend to study, just in case anyone wondered what she was doing there.

Things had come to a sorry state when a person couldn't even use her own bedroom anymore! And, Caroline thought unhappily, it was not going to get any better. It was obvious that she and Chrissy would never get along again. From now on, the kitchen would be her room. She would have to sacrifice the bedroom to Chrissy.

Caroline was so lost in thought that she nearly jumped when her mother walked into the room.

"Hello, Cara. How'd your day go?" Without waiting for a reply, her mother opened a cupboard and began putting the groceries away.

"Great," Caroline murmured. "Just great."

"That's nice, dear. I picked up some Chinese food for dinner. Sound good?"

"Oh. Fine." Her mother didn't even notice that something was bothering her! Didn't anyone notice anything about her anymore? It wasn't bad enough that she was miserable—now she was invisible, too.

"Can you help me set the table?" Her mother set the white cardboard cartons on the counter. "Where's everyone else?"

"I don't know. I just got in myself," Caroline answered.

"Oh. Studying late again?"

"No," Caroline murmured. "I auditioned for something at school."

"That's great. Did you get it?"

Caroline glared at her mother. "Chrissy got it."

"Well, I'm sure you did your best. Wow, Chrissy must be thrilled."

"She's ecstatic," Caroline muttered sarcastically.

Her mother frowned in disapproval. "You're getting an awfully sharp tongue lately, Caroline. I don't think it's very attractive."

"Sorry." Caroline set the table in silence. She usually loved it when they had Chinese food at home, but the fight with Chrissy had ruined her appetite. She doubted she could enjoy anything.

She dropped a plate onto the table and it made a loud clatter. "Are you okay?" her mother asked, peering at her curiously.

"Yes, Mom. Nothing's wrong," Caroline answered methodically.

"Looks like everything's ready," her mother said. "Will you call your father and Chrissy, please?"

Caroline hesitated. "Dad!" she called loudly. "Dinner!" Taking a deep breath, she tried to sound casual. "Dinner, Chrissy," she said.

"She'll never hear you," her mother told her. "Why don't you go get her."

Reluctantly, Caroline started for the bedroom, almost running headlong into Chrissy, who was coming out of the living room.

"Oh." Caroline blushed. "I thought you were in the bedroom."

Chrissy ducked her head. "No. I thought *you* were in the bedroom."

Suddenly Caroline was aware that her mother was watching the two of them carefully. "No, I was in the kitchen," she said quickly.

Avoiding each other's eyes, Caroline and Chrissy took their seats at the table. Caroline's father came in, briskly rubbing his hands together.

"I'm famished. What smells so good?"

"Chinese. Here, Richard. It's your favorite—

shrimp in garlic sauce." Caroline's mother passed him one of the cartons.

Chrissy ate silently with her head down, and Caroline did the same.

"What a boring group we are tonight," her father teased.

"Well, I have interesting news," Mrs. Kirby said. She smiled at all of them. "I've been trying to organize a joint exhibit with the Halloran Gallery, and it's finally come together."

Caroline looked up. "A joint exhibit?"

"Yes. It hasn't been done much in the Bay area, and I'm very excited about it."

Caroline's father nodded. "I get it now. The girls noticed you buttering up Ms. Halloran, and we thought maybe you were angling for a new job."

"Heavens, no! I just wanted her to agree to do this art show. It'll really help both our galleries. We can bring in twice the work, and I hope it'll be a major event. I'm so excited," she repeated.

Caroline stared at Chrissy, who looked like she might have swallowed her sweet and sour chicken the wrong way.

Her mother smiled. "It's funny that you thought I wanted a new job. I'm glad you didn't mention it to anyone." She laughed quietly. "I'd be in big trouble."

Chrissy gulped, her face now turning a sickly purple. "Uh, Aunt Edith—you know that man at the dinner party? Mr. Evans, I think his name was? He was wearing a turtleneck with his suit instead of a regular shirt."

"Frank Evans? I know him very well. He's with the museum."

"Well, uh," Chrissy stuttered nervously, "I sort of,

uh, might have mentioned it to him."

"Mentioned what, Chrissy?" Mrs. Kirby said, as she helped herself to a serving of chicken with cashew nuts.

"That you were interested in working for Ms. Halloran," Chrissy said in a rush. "At least, I think I said that," she added quickly as her aunt's face registered shock. "Just the part about how you were looking for a new job." Chrissy cringed.

"Oh, no! That's just the kind of rumor I was afraid of!"

"I'm sorry," Chrissy apologized. "I had no idea I was wrong. Oh, Aunt Edith—I'd never say anything to get you in trouble! Honest. I'm really, really sorry."

Chrissy was so upset, Caroline almost felt sorry for her.

But her mother pushed back her chair and stood up quickly. "I've got to call the gallery right away. I can't have the whole art community thinking I'm about to change my job."

Chrissy looked miserable. She stared at her plate. "Uncle Richard—I didn't mean to start anything," she whispered. "I'm sorry."

"I can't believe it!" Caroline cried. "Chrissy, you messed up my mother's entire career!"

"Now, go easy on her, Cara," her father said kindly. "She made a mistake and I'm sure she feels terrible about it."

"I do feel awful," Chrissy confessed.

"Maybe no real damage has been done," her father told Chrissy, patting her hand.

"Maybe," Chrissy said, avoiding Caroline's eyes.

Caroline bit her lip. Was Chrissy finally going to get what she deserved?

The minutes crawled by. Caroline could hear her mother's voice in the hall—was she angry or not? Finally, her mother came back into the room.

"I spoke to Ms. Halloran," she said crisply. "And I spoke to my gallery. I've straightened everything out—I hope." She sat down and began eating again as if nothing had happened.

Chrissy's skin was still deeply flushed. "I really am sorry, Aunt Edith," she whispered. "I'll—I'll do anything I can to help."

"You've done enough," her aunt said in a clipped tone.

Chrissy looked so miserable that Caroline couldn't help gloating. *Chrissy deserves this, she really does. She's finally getting a taste of her own medicine.*

In a small voice, Chrissy said, "Aunt Edith . . . I mean it. I'll do anything to help."

"Not now, Chrissy. I'm sure things will work out, but just don't talk to me for a few minutes. I've got to calm down."

Chrissy nodded silently, but a few tears escaped down her cheek. Caroline was surprised to find herself actually feeling sorry for Chrissy. She was used to her mother's ways, but Chrissy wasn't. Caroline knew how awful it felt when her mother turned cold and polite like that: It was worse than if she had exploded. Sometimes, Caroline wished her mother would get really furious and throw a fit for once, instead of inflicting this slow torture when she got mad.

The look on Chrissy's face was almost too much to bear.

"Mom," Caroline blurted, "you know Chrissy didn't mean any harm."

No one said anything. Chrissy was obviously shocked by Caroline coming to her defense. Suddenly Caroline couldn't stop herself—once she'd started, she just kept talking.

"You know how Chrissy is, Mom—she gets so enthusiastic about things. She gets carried away. She didn't mean to hurt you."

Her mother pursed her lips. "Thoughtlessness is no excuse. You two are old enough to be responsible for the things you say."

"I know we are," Caroline heard herself answer, "but you said yourself no one had heard any rumors. So there's been no harm done."

"That's true." Her mother relaxed in her chair. "I suppose I gave you a hard time, Chrissy."

Chrissy smiled shyly. "That's okay, Aunt Edith. I understand. I—I know I talk too much sometimes, but I don't mean to upset anybody." She glanced at Caroline, then looked back at her aunt. "I'm just so glad you can forgive me. I really am sorry, and I would just hate it if you were angry and—"

"That's enough," Mrs. Kirby interrupted. She leaned her head on her hand and looked right at Chrissy. "My word, Chrissy, you talk enough for three people! I suppose I'll just have to learn to get used to it."

"So will I," added Caroline. She smiled warmly at Chrissy. It wasn't much, she thought, but it was a start.

* * *

A pleasant breeze ruffled the curtains. Caroline leaned her head back on her pillow with a sigh of contentment. She and Chrissy were peacefully co-existing in the same bedroom. They hadn't spoken much, but then again, they hadn't argued, either.

"Cara—can we talk for a minute?" Chrissy asked all of a sudden. "I—I have a confession to make."

"No, *I* have a confession to make," Caroline insisted. "I'm so glad we're talking again, Chrissy. I was angry at you, but not for a good reason, It was only all the attention you were getting. I was so jealous."

"So was I!" Chrissy exclaimed. "I was jealous of *you.*"

"Of me?" Caroline gaped at her. "But why?"

"Oh, Cara, I know it was wrong, but I couldn't help myself. You have things so much easier. Nothing bad ever happens to your family. You have a beautiful home, and nice clothes . . . I envy them. And I'm ashamed of myself for envying them. My family gives me everything they can, plus a lot of love. I don't need anything more. But I wanted it."

Caroline spoke slowly. "I know how you feel, Chrissy. It's hard to want things you can't have. But, you know, my family has problems, too. They're different, that's all."

"I know," Chrissy said, "but I couldn't help it. I wanted to be like you. I—I wanted to *be* you."

Caroline was taken aback. "You're kidding, right?"

"You have so much, Cara."

"But Chrissy—there are so many reasons why *I* envy *you.*"

"There are?" Chrissy looked amazed.

"Of course. Your family is so close and open—not in the least like mine. I wish we were more like yours."

"So we were both wrong," Chrissy said quietly. "But Cara, I hate what I did. Part of me did want to compete against you—and win."

"Oh, Chrissy." Caroline bit her lip.

"I knew you wanted to run the senior committee, but I did, too. Try to see it my way—I still feel like an outsider. I just wanted to belong."

"But you do belong," Caroline insisted. "In some ways, more than me. People take to you immediately, Chrissy. I have to work harder."

"But that doesn't make me any more sure of myself," Chrissy protested. "I still don't feel I belong here."

"That's how I feel at school." Caroline paused. "Maybe everyone feels that way sometimes."

"Maybe—but I live in your house," Chrissy pointed out. "My friends are mostly your friends. I just wanted one thing to be all my own."

Caroline frowned. "We both wanted something of our own."

"I guess I was pretty selfish," Chrissy said finally. "But I never planned to hurt you! You have to believe me. It was all an accident."

"There were a lot of pretty painful accidents," Caroline said softly.

"But they just happened. Please believe me. Like, with Tracy and Tony—the model ship scheme just popped into my head."

Caroline grinned in spite of herself. "It was pretty funny, actually. And it worked."

Chrissy grinned, too. "We'll have to wait and see

about that. If it backfires, Tracy will be really mad at me."

"I'd like to forgive you, Chrissy," Caroline said sincerely, "but it's hard. These last weeks I felt like I had no one to turn to. Not Tracy, or you, or even my own mother."

"I'm sorry about that, too. I'm almost glad she got mad at me tonight."

"It certainly cleared the air," Caroline admitted, chuckling.

"Cara—I have another confession. Your mother never told me anything about wanting a new job. That day we went shopping together, your mom called Ms. Halloran and I overheard and took things the wrong way."

Caroline rolled her eyes. "That's just like you."

"Yeah, I guess. Your mom was right to be furious with me. I could have started awful rumors."

"But you didn't," Caroline assured Chrissy. "And she wasn't half as mad as she looked. You know how she is—she gets that way with me, too, sometimes."

"Still—would you put in a good word for me with her, Cara?"

"Sure, but I don't think you'll need it."

Chrissy sighed in relief. "And another thing." Chrissy took a deep breath. "Don't ever make me go shopping alone with your mother again," she blurted.

"But I thought you liked it!"

"I did, but she's so stubborn. And, well, we don't really have the same taste. When she wanted one thing, I wanted the opposite. You should have seen us—like two ornery mules trying to pull the same cart in two directions. It was *not* a pretty sight."

Caroline burst out laughing. "Come on, you're exaggerating."

Chrissy grinned. "A little. But shopping is much more fun when you're along. Everything is more fun when you're there."

"I feel the same way about you," Caroline cried.

"And you don't hate me?" Chrissy asked timidly.

"I never hated you! I was just angry when I said that. I didn't mean it, but I was hurt."

Chrissy nodded knowingly. "It's only human to feel that way sometimes—that's what my mom always told me."

"I feel so much better now," Caroline exclaimed. Then she paused: there was one more thing she needed to explain.

"Chrissy, I really feel terrible about your house being destroyed. I know how much you wanted to go back home this year."

Chrissy sighed. "I really did, Cara. I'm starting to think I'll never fit in there again and it's so scary. I'll have nothing in common with my old friends in Iowa, but I'll never be a true San Franciscan either."

"You don't have to be," Caroline said warmly. "You're *you*—a true original. You fit in anywhere."

"Cara, don't be so nice to me! I feel ashamed! I did such awful things to you. Look, how about if I resign from the committee," Chrissy promised. "And we'll hold auditions for Skit Night emcee again. You're right, it wasn't fair. You should have won."

"No, don't do that," Caroline said sheepishly. "I, um, I really don't want to run the committee anymore."

"You don't?" Chrissy stared in surprise.

"I don't want to give up my acting class. I really like it, and I need all my spare time for it." Caroline's eyes shone with excitement.

"You really mean it?" Chrissy marveled. "You're happy with the way things are?"

"More than I knew, at first." Caroline smiled. "So don't feel bad. The committee thing has worked out for the best."

"But what about emcee?"

Caroline grew thoughtful. "I did want to be emcee, but I'm not going to be a spoilsport. Everyone wanted you. You should do it."

Chrissy smacked a hand against her forehead. "Holy mazoley, Cara, what have we been thinking? You're an actress! Let's come up with an absolutely fantastic skit for you! Then we can really spotlight your talents like you deserve. Cara, you'll be the star of the show!"

"You're right," Caroline exclaimed. "I didn't even think of that." Her eyes widened in excitement. "I could still use all those jokes Zach taught me."

"It would be hilarious," Chrissy agreed.

Caroline hesitated. "Chrissy, not that I'm worried, but . . . you won't change your mind this time, will you? Or try to steal the show?"

"Don't even *think* that," Chrissy said heatedly. "But Cara," she added, looking a bit sheepish, "just in case I forget, and get all excited about another idea . . . this time, will you remind me? You have to promise to bring me back to earth when I get carried away like that."

"I will. I promise."

"We should never ever fight again," Chrissy declared. She brightened. "I know—let's ask Tracy to help with skit ideas. Three heads are better than one." She leaped out of bed and sat at Caroline's side.

Caroline threw her arms around her cousin. "It's great to be friends again."

"It's the best," Chrissy agreed.

"And I have this feeling," Caroline said, "that from now on, senior year will be the best year we ever had."

Here's a sneak preview of *Make Me a Star*, book number ten in the continuing SUGAR & SPICE series from Ivy Books.

Chrissy's heart started pounding harder and faster. Her time to be discovered had nearly come! *I've just got to make a good impression,* she thought as she stared intently at the door of the gym where the auditions were being held. The director's assistant came out and set his clipboard down on the step while he gave directions to one of the other girls. Curious, Chrissy sat quietly on the step, determined to take a look. *It's a schedule for filming,* Chrissy thought, as she scanned the top page marked "Extras." Underneath it was the shooting schedule for the next few days. Her eyes caught the entry for the following afternoon. Sunday. 3:00. The Japanese Tea Garden, Golden Gate Park.

"Let's go, Chrissy," called Caroline as their group lined up for the audition. Chrissy darted back to her place in line behind Caroline and the girls walked through the expansive double doors of the gymnasium. Nervously, the girls marched down the center line as they had been instructed. On one side of the bleachers, a long table and several chairs had been set up. Immediately, Chrissy recognized the director, Justin Hayes, sitting in the center, flanked by the young stars, Pete Becker and Nick Matthews. Chrissy turned to face the panel, trying not to let her knees shake.

ABOUT THE AUTHOR

Janet Quin-Harkin is the author of more than thirty books for young adults, including the best-selling *Ten-Boy Summer* and *On Our Own*, its sequel series. Ms. Quin-Harkin lives just outside of San Francisco with her husband, three teenage daughters, and one son.